Allison M. Azulay

IN THE FAST LANE

Coffee Break Collection 4

Copyright © 2019 by Allison M. Azulay. All rights reserved.

The use of any part of this publication, reproduced, transmitted in any form or by any means electronic, mechanical, photocopying, recording or otherwise, or stored in a retrieval system without the prior written consent of the publisher is an infringement of the copyright law, except in the case of brief quotations embodied in critical articles and reviews.

The stories in this volume are works of fiction. Names, characters, places and incidents are products of the author's imagination or are used fictitiously. Any resemblance to actual events or locales or persons, living or dead, is entirely coincidental.

https://www.allison-m-azulay.ca

ISBN 978-1-989215-79-1 (softcover)

Cover design by
SelfPubBookCovers.com/Acapellabookcoverdesign

Published by Allison M. Azulay
in Renfrew, Ontario, Canada

Table of Contents

Karma 1

    Chapter 1 3

    Chapter 2 14

    Chapter 3 21

    Chapter 4 29

    Chapter 5 36

    Chapter 6 44

    Chapter 7 52

    Chapter 8 60

    Chapter 9 65

    Chapter 10 69

    Chapter 11 75

    Chapter 12 80

    Chapter 13 89

    Chapter 14 97

    Chapter 15 103

CYBER PRINCE CHARMING 109

    CHAPTER 1 111

    CHAPTER 2 124

CHAPTER 3	136
CHAPTER 4	145
CHAPTER 5	152
CHAPTER 6	157
CHAPTER 7	168
CHAPTER 8	181
CHAPTER 9	185
CHAPTER 10	189
CHAPTER 11	200
CHAPTER 12	206
ACKNOWLEDGEMENTS	213
Other Books by Allison M. Azulay	215
about the author	216

Karma

Chapter 1

MISTAKES

I SHOULD HAVE KNOWN. Terry was a schmuck at the best of times, and these were by no means the best of times. He was headed for rehab, and he asked a couple of us to take his gigs while he cleaned out. I agreed. I should have known better.

OLDER WOMEN had always been my specialty. Not that I liked them any more than I liked the younger ones; I just found it easier to play the game with them. And they knew the score; so, most never expected more than I could give. A few suggested marriage—a boy toy they could have at their beck and call—but I made it clear I wanted no strings, and all save one settled for regular visits and the odd weekend in the Caribbean or Switzerland. That one persistent old broad, though, was a whiney pain in the ass for a year before a stroke took her and ended my torment.

Yeah, I know. I'm a heartless bastard. You have to be in this business. And I suppose I come by it naturally, thanks to my mother and her "friends."

Friends. Mom never had a friend in her life. She used people and that's a fact. She used me, and that's a fact, too. Not that I minded, at first. Hell, at fifteen, getting laid regularly was a kid's dream come true. And we did need the money.

I was already tall at twelve and grew to six-foot-four, so I tend to stand out in a crowd. Muscular even as a teenager, well tanned, with black hair I keep long and tied at my nape. And I'm handsome; all my ladies tell me with their eyes if not their words.

But Mom was my first. She called it "training" and, for all it felt great, it also felt...unnatural. Wrong. I guess that's why I numbed myself inside. It was the only way I could get it up with her after that first time. And once she started bringing customers home, I avoided her as best I could. But she had needs, and I was the only guy available back then.

But that's all old news and I don't think about it much anymore.

I suppose you could say I forgave her. Not that I ever really begrudged her in the first place. I even went to her funeral. She'd overdosed along with her latest man, and the two had lain in the dump they lived in for a week before somebody finally decided to find out what that smell was.

I hadn't seen her for years; that's why I hadn't realized she was using. I'd been sending her cash every month, not knowing I was feeding the habit that would kill her. I guess some would call that karma.

But like I said, that's all old news and not my problem.

The present: Now, that's my problem.

IT HAD ALL SEEMED NORMAL ENOUGH, though "normal" is not a word that remotely applies. The agency texted me to take a plane to Washington and wired me the tickets and reservations for a hotel in D.C. *Normally*, I stay as far from that hellhole as I can. A nest of sickos and weirdos, that town, just like L.A. and New York—and that's not counting the perverts. Three places I don't even like to visit, much less work in. Just sitting in the airport on a layover makes me want to take a long shower.

But I'd promised Terry I'd take his regulars and, for all he was an asshole, he was the only friend I had. Besides, the boss was still pissed at me for refusing a poor-little-rich-girl out of Chicago looking for action during her vacation in the south. The sonofabitch had finally admitted I was right: She was underage. But the new management (the company I'd signed on with years ago got bought out a few months back) doesn't give a damn about precautions; they're just in it for the money. And while I'd already decided to go independent, I needed extra cash to tide me over till I established myself in another city.

So, when I got the call to take one of Terry's out-of-town specials, I figured I could make an exception to my personal rule this one time.

Should have known better.

THE ADDRESS I RECEIVED BY TEXT took me to a rundown section of Georgetown full of abandoned three-storey houses that had once been the elegant town homes of politicians and magnates. It didn't surprise me that I'd been directed here, because I'd read that a program of rehabilitation had been initiated and many a junior politician and bureaucrat was taking advantage of the low prices for the fixer-uppers.

I passed the brownstone at a crawl, checking it out, and I noticed a light on upstairs, on the second floor. No illumination anywhere else, but I figured she was alone and getting herself ready for me. So I continued on around the block and checked the time on my dash. Couple of minutes yet. I eased to the edge of the alley, turned off the headlights, and cut the engine.

I wanted a cigarette. But I'd been trying to quit and I hadn't brought any with me; so, I just stepped out of the car, locked it, and walked around to the front entrance.

Most of the houses were dark. Only two at the end of the block, on the opposite side of the street, appeared inhabited. Good. It wouldn't do to have some concerned citizen trying to rescue a client who didn't want rescuing. That was the problem with rape fantasies: If she played up her victimhood too well, there was always a chance the cops would be called in and I'd spend a night in an interrogation room trying to explain it was all just a game. Back in Miami, they knew me and didn't trouble me anymore. But this was terra incognita and I could end up in the slammer if the woman backtracked out of embarrassment and denied having hired me. Another reason I shouldn't have come here.

With a last look around, I climbed the steps, rang the bell three times, and waited. A minute later, the porch light turned on and the door opened. I blinked in shock: Instead of dressing the siren in filmy negligé and strappy sandals, this woman wore flannelette pyjamas under a terrycloth robe, rags tied in her grey-streaked brown hair, and fluffy bunny slippers that had seen a few years' use. She was short, maybe five-four, tops, and her squarish face bore ordinary features and pale eyes that looked green in the light of the lamp that overhung the door. She wore no makeup and seemed tired.

It took me a moment to process her unexpected dishevelment, and I ignored the vague familiarity that a voice in the back of my mind noted.

Her words brought me out of my stupor.

"Can I help you?"

Slipping into game mode, I pushed in as I

said, "Yes, you can, sweetheart."

Her eyes flew wide and she gaped at me as I held her arms and pressed her back. I kicked the door shut behind me, and I walked her to the nearest wall to plant her there and lift her enough to kiss her.

She didn't resist, at first. Then, she started to struggle and emit frightened squeaks of protest. Alarm bells rang in my head, but I dismissed them and persisted in my role as I groped her roughly per the instructions texted to me.

She tasted good, and I'd risen to the occasion already. That was unusual: Generally, I had to work myself up to an erection, which had the benefit of giving me plenty of time for the foreplay that pleasured the customer and guaranteed repeat performances. But something about this dowdy little woman had me aching for her before I'd even gotten the scruffy robe untied. Strange, what turns a man on.

It was not the increasing urgency of her efforts to push me away or the swelling volume of her screams that gave me pause. It was the tears.

I stopped and pulled back, breathing raggedly with the desire I had not anticipated.

Those tears gleamed in the pale light of the exterior carriage lamp that shone through the transom above the door and the curtainless leaded-glass window nearby. She stood trembling and sobbing. I let go of her and stepped back, suddenly not sure this was an act. Not sure I even had the right address.

"Excuse me, Ma'am. Is this one-two-five Mary Street? Are you Sarah Wagner?"

She blinked and frowned perplexedly.

"Uh, yes." Said with hesitance.

It struck me to ask, "And you hired me?"

Her frown deepened.

"Hired you for what? I didn't hire anyone." Her tone sharpened with anger and indignation. "And if I had, that gives you no right to assault me!"

"Oh, crap!" I said on a breath. "What the hell is going on?"

"That's what I'd like to know. But...but...I want you to leave. Now." She straightened, elongating her neck, pointing to the door, and pursing her mouth in an adorable expression of dignified command.

God, I wanted her!

But something was very wrong about the whole situation, and my instinct for survival warred with my urge to sow my seed. I stepped back again to put distance between us in hope of quelling the lust I couldn't explain.

"Look, I know this is going to sound preposterous, but I was hired by someone to show you a good time."

She blinked at me in bewilderment. Then, she demanded, "What are you talking about? How is what you did showing me a good time? And who hired you?"

I sighed. "I thought you hired me, but apparently that's not the case."

"No it is not."

"Well, someone did. And I was told you wanted a rape scenario."

In outrage, she shrilled, "Why would I want such a thing?"

I couldn't help smiling at her naïveté. "Some women do. Maybe a psychologist could tell you why."

She pondered the notion a moment, her eyes searching the floor, before she looked to me once more. Her respirations slowed and deepened and she swallowed. She concluded, "Somebody wanted you to hurt me."

"Maybe," I allowed. "But if I say so myself, my clients usually come away satisfied."

"Your clients," she repeated. "You're a...."

When she didn't finish, I supplied the word. "A gigolo. A prostitute."

Her faint response: "Yes. I see."

Tears flooded her cheeks and I gaped at her.

"What's wrong?" I wondered as though everything was not.

She forced a smile and straightened, pressing her lips tightly as she struggled to control herself. At last, she wiped her cheeks and eyes and said, "Never mind. Doesn't matter."

At that moment, all I wanted to do was wrap her in my arms and comfort her. Well, that and get her into bed. But my brain had gone into overdrive trying to figure out what was happening and what to do about it. At a suspicion, I crept to the window, staying back against the wall, and I scanned the street. My gut and hands clenched at sight of a van parked across the way and one house up. Another pulled behind it. And a third passed out of view, slowing as it did.

"Damn!" I whispered.

"What?"

"News crews."

She gasped.

Keeping to the shadows, I slid back to her and suggested, "Maybe you'd better get dressed. I'll check the back and see if we can get out of here unnoticed."

"Why should I run? This is my home."

With a wry smile, I told her, "Honey, you can bet your last dollar you were filmed letting me into your house."

"But I didn't!"

Waving dismissal of the protest, I said, "You know it and I know it, but whoever set us up will make sure no one believes that." I added, "And frankly, I don't want to go to prison to protect your reputation, even if it would help."

Her face fell.

"Look," I said gently, "just go get dressed while I find a way out of this."

She nodded unhappily and trudged to a door that must have led to the staircase.

Chapter 2

ESCAPE

I ROVED THE EMPTY LOWER ROOMS to peer through bare windows into the D.C. dusk.

"Idiot!" I berated myself under my breath. "Why the hell didn't I dump this one on Vince? This is his burg."

He'd have raped her and not given a flying fuck until he had to go on the lam, a voice in my head reminded me. Somebody Upstairs must be looking out for this broad. So, lucky me, I get to play hero.

Hero. Right. I really didn't have a clue

how to fix it. All I could come up with was to get away somewhere, away from reporters, to buy time to think it through and make a plan.

I expelled a resigned breath as I moved on to the kitchen and located the back door. It was Dutch style, the upper half glazed. I carefully pulled back the gingham curtain just a tad and panned the yard. No sign of movement. I squinted into the darkness beyond the garage, but saw nothing. Unfortunately, I knew too well that didn't mean a damn thing. Who knew how many were hiding out there? I'd already missed at least one camera in front.

Only one thing to do, I decided. I unlocked and opened the door and strode out as though I was just out for a breath of fresh air. (Not that D.C. air could be described as fresh.) I stood at the edge of the small porch, inhaled deeply, stretched my arms, curled them in again, and twisted from the waist. Then, I descended to the grass and strolled in the intermittent starlight, blatantly flexing muscles along the way as I glanced about. The tall fence hid much beyond it from view; so, I continued to the rear gate. Turning, I scanned the houses to left and right of the not-client's and then pivoted to study those across the back lane. A lamp in an upper window two doors down revealed a man on a treadmill.

I flipped the lock, pressed the latch, and swung the gate open. Somewhere near, a dog barked as a car rolled by and disappeared past the next bend, its headlights glinting off my rented black Jaguar on the right and a silver Lexus on the left. The service alley looked empty, but the raised hairs on the back of my neck told me not to trust appearances. On impulse, I jogged to the Jag and climbed in to open the glove box. As I made a show of searching the box, the dash, and the front seat for something, I swept the area now illuminated by the car's interior light. A slight motion in the hedge one house over caught my eye. Damn! I knew it! I exited the Jag, locked it, pretended to put something into my shirt pocket—like I'd forgotten my condoms—and strode back through the gate and into the house.

THE WOMAN HAD COME DOWN in a dress and jacket, a purse slung over her shoulder and her hair brushed.

"Have you got your passport?" I asked her.

"I'm not leaving the country," she said. "Besides, I don't have one."

I insisted, "The point is, don't leave anything important behind. Pack light, but pack as though you'll never come back."

"You're scaring me."

"Good. You should be scared," I said. "Don't underestimate anybody who would go to such lengths to smear you." It occurred to me to wonder, "Who are you, exactly?"

"Well, uh, I'm the new representative for Minnesota."

"Of course!" I exclaimed, hitting my head in realization. "That explains it!"

"It does?"

I stared at her in disbelief. "You can't really be that naïve, can you?" I pointed out, "You've already pissed off more than a few people with your questions about Congressman Jackson's bill." (I'd read the latest buzz on the plane to Washington.)

She blushed and dropped her eyes, pressing her lips so tightly they blanched.

Aware I'd embarrassed her, I said, "Look, I'm sorry. I don't mean to offend you. But we're both in real trouble, here." I pulled out my cell phone. "What's the number of the house behind you?"

"I don't know their phone number."

"I meant the house number."

"Oh. One twenty-five, same as mine."

As I googled D.C. taxis, I reminded her, "Go pack what you need for a few days away. Like I said, bring everything you don't want stolen or destroyed."

Wishing I'd taken similar precautions tonight, I hoped I'd be able to clear out my hotel room.

She hurried upstairs. I ordered a cab for the lane behind 125 Nadine.

BUSHES ALONG THE ALLEY came alive when we dashed to the cab and slid into the back seat before the driver could stop us.

"I'm not here for you," the man objected.

"Yes, you are," I told him. "I got my streets mixed up, that's all. Now, get us out of here, fast." Camera flashes lit the night as I handed him a hundred-dollar bill.

"Okay," the driver responded, wrapping bill and hand around the steering wheel and stomping the gas pedal. "Going anywhere in particular, folks?" he asked as he swerved around a man with a Nikon.

"We'll start with the downtown Hilton," I replied.

"Why there?" my fellow fugitive asked.

My smile sardonic, I said, "Forgot my passport."

IT AMUSED THE DRIVER that I asked him to drop me at the service entrance. I suppose he'd seen his share of shenanigans in the nation's capital. Leaving Ms. Wagner and another hundred, I ducked into the hotel kitchen and wove among the handful of startled cooks and waiters on the night shift and then followed a maid to one of the remote elevators used more frequently by staff than by patrons. Up I rode to the eighteenth floor. At this hour, the halls were empty but for me and the maid who took extra towels to an aging Texan two doors from my room. When he answered her knock, I recognized the big cowboy who had booked in the same time I did. He looked me over and nodded as I passed, before he closed himself in.

After a quick survey of the suite to determine if anything had been moved, I hastily gathered my belongings into my overnight bag. On my way out, I glanced to my key card and considered whether to return it to the concierge. No, I decided. I slid it into my pocket and strode to the rearmost stairwell.

Seventeen flights down, I exited the hotel, climbed into the cab, and ordered, "Take us to the airport."

I SAT SIDEWAYS AND WATCHED the traffic behind. No vehicle behaved in a way that suggested we were being followed, but I kept an eye out anyway. It was as much habit as a response to the current circumstance: I'd escorted my share of celebrities and knew how easy it was to be caught unawares by fanatical fans, predatory paparazzi, or suspicious spouses.

Finally, we pulled onto the access ramp and around to the airport entrance.

Another tip to the driver, and in we went to weave among travellers negotiating the long building. The terminal never slept, and we queued up at the ticket counter to take the first flight out. Even here, I scanned for sign of pursuit. I relaxed only when we boarded the plane.

Chapter 3

DESPERATE MEASURES

ALMOST EVERY SEAT ON THE RED-EYE had been taken, but we managed to squeeze into a pair in the last row, next to the toilets. Most of the passengers dozed, but my companion and I were both too wound up to sleep.

"I don't see why we're going to Las Vegas," she whispered.

"We're going to get married," I murmured with a grin.

She blinked at me a moment and then chuckled dismissively. Finally, she pulled a magazine from the pouch behind the seat before her and began to pass the time reading. I watched her, marvelling that she trusted me—a total stranger who had almost raped her—enough to just go along blindly with whatever I chose to do.

I guessed she'd come to the same conclusion I had: that whoever was behind all this wanted to either control her vote in the House (she was an Independent) or to discredit her enough to force her resignation in favour of someone malleable. Of course, I was just a pawn. Collateral damage. No one would give a damn what happened to a man like me.

I leaned back in my seat. She thought I was kidding about marriage. And I had, in fact, been joking when I said it; the truth was I'd chosen Vegas on impulse, just figuring it beat Detroit.

But the more I thought about it, the more I realized marrying this woman was the solution to her problem and to mine. And the more I thought about it, the more obscure the future became in my imagination. Marriage was uncharted territory. I'd never once considered it an option. Yet here I was: on the matrimonial path. Would we divorce in a year or so? Likely.

We were absolute strangers and, from what I saw of her, absolute opposites. The chances were we'd detest each other in short order. And even if our relations remained amicable, the odds were that we'd find it easier to live apart than together.

I wondered if she had money, but a discreet perusal of her poly jacket, out-of-date cotton jersey dress, and well-worn shoes told me she'd be lucky to have two dimes to rub together. Then, I remembered an article about her unexpected victory in the special election that followed the death of the old codger who had represented his state and district for nigh on thirty years: Sarah Wagner was an unmarried diner waitress who lived in a trailer park, and no one had given her bid for the Congressional seat a second thought. Until, that is, she won by a landslide. Since then, speculation as to how a nobody who had done nothing to seek votes could win against two well-known and well-heeled candidates had run from fixing of the election to voting-machine malfunction to mass voter protest of the mudslinging that had characterized her opponents' campaigns. I'd place my bet on the last.

The reporter had spent half his article

enumerating the debates and door-knocking and speeches and interviews into which the other two hopefuls had poured time and effort and money to appeal to the electorate. Ms. Wagner, on the other hand, had not made one speech, participated in any debate, given a single interview. The public had not known there was a third candidate until voting day.

Now, here she was, a rookie member of Congress being attacked after only one month in office.

"Why did you run?" I heard myself ask aloud.

She looked to me and blushed again.

"I didn't."

I frowned. "Come again?"

"I didn't," she repeated. With a deep breath, she explained, "Since I was in grade school, there has been this one girl who always made fun of me. Of my clothes, my hair, my home, my parents. She liked to play tricks on me. Why she picked on me in particular I have never known, but she has bullied me since the first day we met.

"I can't prove it, but I know she's the one who put my name in. She must have forged my signature and paid the fees. I think she figured she'd make me a laughingstock for presuming to run for office and then getting no votes."

I frowned as I mulled her confession. "When did you find out you were a candidate?"

"Election day. Same as everybody else." She added, "I haven't seen her since I won; she's probably fuming and trying to get even. But she needn't bother: I'm way over my head. I spent all my savings getting here and getting a place to live. I've had to scour thrift shops to put together a wardrobe good enough to wear on Capitol Hill—all I had was diner uniforms and jeans. And I end every day with a headache trying to read and understand the mountains of paperwork that land on my desk."

I wondered, "How is she getting even?"

She allowed, "Well, maybe it's not all her doing. But my Washington staff quit the week I got here. Administration has delayed my pay so I have no income, yet, and I can barely afford to buy groceries. Over half the district-office staff quit this past week. Yes, some were due to retire anyway, but all in one week?"

She snorted a bitter chuckle. "I hear about how Congressmen get all these free lunches and free dinners and other stuff. I haven't seen a one."

With another huff, she said, "I can't even afford a secretary to sort my mail, right now, because of a mix-up over my Representational Allowance. But the newspapers in my home town claim I'm living high on the public dime — and that, I'm sure, is her doing."

With a grimacing smile, she raised sorrowful eyes to mine, and my heart ached for her. She'd had a tough life full of bad luck that had just gotten worse. Maybe we weren't as different as I thought.

SHE STEPPED OUT OF THE CAB and stopped dead, her eyes owlish as she gazed up at the glittering hotel-casino that soared into the dawn sky. I chuckled as I grasped her hand and pulled her to the entrance.

"Can you afford this?" she gasped. "'Cause I sure can't!"

"For a week or two," I assured her. "But we won't be here that long."

As I dragged her along to check in, she staggered and stumbled, gaping in awe and swivelling all about to take in every detail of the sumptuous decor and stylish clientele. I stifled a chuckle at her wonderment. My own fascination with such glamour had died long ago.

"Is the honeymoon suite available?" I

asked the blue-suited woman at the desk.

Sarah whirled and blinked at me, astonished, as the clerk punched commands into her computer.

An instant later, the young woman replied apologetically, "I'm afraid they're all booked, sir." She added, "But one is free for the next three days, if you don't mind cutting your stay short. We could move you to another room on Saturday." She looked to Sarah, and her face registered shock at the age of the woman standing with me.

"Perfect," I said. "Three days is all we'll need."

Sarah's increasingly uncertain gaze jumped from me to the clerk and back, but she said nothing. And the young brunette smiled uncomfortably before encoding our room key.

AN HOUR LATER, Sarah balked when we emerged from the cab before the little chapel on Newton Avenue. Her eyes took on the wild look of a cornered animal.

I clasped her hand and squeezed. "It'll be over before you know it," I told her as though we were entering a dentist's office to have her teeth extracted.

"No, I don't think...I-I—"

"Don't think," I urged. "Just say, 'I do.'"

She turned terrified eyes to me. Locking them, I pulled her hand to kiss her knuckles and then smiled and winked at her before drawing her inside.

The officiant and his wife beamed beatifically and a young woman handed flowers to Sarah when we presented ourselves for the ceremony that would bind us as husband and wife. My intended glanced about dazedly throughout the choosing of the ring from the selection conveniently offered and the performance of the rite, a peculiar fact not lost on the Reverend and Mrs. Bailey. I suspect Sarah was trying to convince herself it was all just a strange dream.

As for me, it was the signing of the documents to make it legal that tensed my gut with the recognition that this was, effectively, for keeps. Nonetheless, I pushed my mouth into a smile as the Baileys and their daughter congratulated us, and I tried my best to project confidence, if not happiness, to my bride.

All the way back to the hotel, Sarah cried.

Chapter 4

HONEYMOON

EVERYONE WE PASSED smiled with sympathy in response to Sarah's red eyes, wet cheeks, and obvious distress, probably assuming she'd lost all her savings at the tables. As we waited before the elevator among milling patrons on their way to their own rooms, a young woman leaned close and murmured, "Maybe a show will cheer your mother. The upper lounge has the music people of her generation like to hear." The blonde smiled benignly, certain of the helpfulness of her suggestion. But Sarah was not deaf, and she sobbed the harder at the insult the younger woman had not intended.

I sighed. This was not going as I'd hoped. Perhaps I should have consulted my bride before marrying her, I thought. Maybe I should have calmly laid out my reasoning and the options open to us once we tied the knot. After all, we need live together only a few months. A year, tops. Then, we could separate awhile and file for divorce as soon as our apparent marital difficulties had ceased to be newsworthy. While the press and public might question her wisdom in wedding me, they would surely consider her justified in ending the marriage when I gave her cause. Easy peasy. Her reputation remains intact, I stay out of jail, and the whole matter blows over in a week or two.

But as I opened the door to our suite, her face and a feeling in my gut told me this would not be as simple as I supposed.

ROOM SERVICE DELIVERED the breakfast I'd ordered on the way up. We ate in silence punctuated by her sniffles and the scrape of utensils on china. Well, *I* ate; she barely touched her fruit cup.

She no longer wept; she'd lapsed into a sullen stupor. And I felt the more miserable for it.

I returned from setting the trays outside the door to find her lying on the far side of the enormous bed, still dressed, and curled on top of the pink satin comforter, her back to me.

Not knowing what else to do, I crawled over to lie next to her. Hesitantly, I closed the gap between us to spoon with her. Then, I reached my arm around and waited for her response. She heaved a shuddering sigh.

I inched closer still until our bodies met and I felt her warmth through all the layers of our garments. I drank in the scent of her, and my cock stiffened as I savoured the heady perfume that set me throbbing. What was it about her that aroused me? I wondered as I nuzzled her neck and pulled her tighter against me.

"You don't have to pretend you want me."

The words took a moment to sink in. When they did, I moved back enough to pull her around to face me.

"Does this feel like I'm pretending?" I demanded as I grabbed her hand and forced it to my phallus.

Her eyes welled. "It's your job, isn't it? Making yourself excited enough to...." Her breath caught as she tried not to sob. "Even if you don't really want to."

I grasped her chin a little too firmly. "Listen to me," I commanded. "Yes, I can get it up even when I don't feel any attraction to a woman. I can make it happen. But I don't have to force it with you."

She smiled sadly. "Yeah."

I knew she meant, "You say that to all your clients." And she was right; I do. But for once it was true. For lack of anything to convince her, I simply kissed her.

Now, I was losing it. I wanted her more than I'd ever wanted a woman in my life. I didn't know why and I didn't care. I had to have her. Now.

Her clothes were in the way and I couldn't get them off fast enough. I ripped at the buttons as I tasted her hungrily and I yanked off jacket and skirt, blouse and pantyhose, camisole and panties. My own skin needed to touch hers, and I wrenched off my shirt to send buttons flying. I got the slacks down just enough to free my cock and I pushed inside her.

At her cry, I stopped partway, panting, and I realized she wasn't wet enough. And she was damn tight, too. For the first time since my youth, I'd failed to put my partner's pleasure first. That recognition should have been enough to deflate me, but it didn't. Nevertheless, I couldn't proceed without making it worth her while. More than ever before, I truly wanted to please this woman. Not as a matter of pride in skill, but because I needed her to enjoy me as much as I enjoyed her.

"I'm sorry," I apologized. "I got too excited." I kissed her tenderly. "I promise I'll make it up to you."

It was then I noticed the fear in her eyes.

"I won't hurt you," I told her earnestly, suddenly afraid my fervour would drive her away. "I swear I won't hurt you again. Never."

"You're-you're-you're...you're too big," she stammered through frightened sobs.

At that, I leaned on one elbow and cupped her cheek. "No," I murmured. "I just haven't made you ready, yet." I kissed her left eye, then her right, then her lips. "But I will."

With that, I pushed myself up and finished stripping off the last of my clothing, all the while gazing at her. My bold stare disconcerted her and she pulled the comforter to wrap herself.

"No," I said as I tossed it back to bare her.

"No. I want to look at you."

"I'm not much to look at," she said diffidently.

"Who told you that?" I replied, irritated that anyone would depreciate a woman that way. As I traced her pale, round form with my eyes, I declared, "You're lovely, Sarah."

Her expression showed her insecurity, but I determined to prove my appreciation. I slid between her legs and claimed every inch of her from head to toe and back.

And then I made her want me.

MY HEART GRADUALLY SLOWED as I lay with her in my arms. Her. Sarah. My wife. It felt both strange and wondrous to think of her as mine. No woman had ever been my own before. They had always been on loan from the husband they already had or the next man they would take. I'd always been just a momentary pleasure. A disposable toy. Even those who had urged me to marry them had only wanted a permanent lover waiting when they tired of other fancies.

But Sarah was mine. Completely. I hadn't realized until I felt her hymen that she was a virgin. I'd never encountered one, before, and in this day and age I had not expected to. I wondered how it was that a woman of her years had never had a man. Not that I minded at all. In fact, it thrilled me to know I was her first.

I regarded her where she slumbered at my shoulder. The white filaments scattered among her shoulder-length brown locks glistened in the late morning sunshine that flooded the room. Fine lines surrounded her eyes and deeper ones bracketed her mouth. My gaze drifted from the rose pink of her lips, over the fair skin of her neck and breasts, to the matching pink of her nipples, and on across the slightly rounded belly to the brown fur below.

Just looking at her hardened me again. I couldn't imagine ever having enough of her.

Chapter 5

MARRIED LIFE

THREE DAYS FLEW BY and it wasn't near enough time to enjoy each other. But we needed to get back to D.C. I booked us on another Red-Eye to minimize the likelihood anyone would notice our return. My bride slept all the way across the continent. (I have to admit I'd kept her awake for most of those three days.)

We arrived by cab at Mary Street and I saw Sarah into the brownstone early Sunday before taking the Jag back to the airport and flying to Miami. In Florida, I emptied my accounts, packed my belongings (just wardrobe and toiletries), closed my apartment, handed in my notice, and said goodbye to Terry. I got back to Georgetown in time to watch the sun rise with Sarah on Monday morning.

I provided cab fare and sent her to the Hill well ahead of her usual arrival so she could slip into her office on the sly. It would be a long day for her, I knew: Reporters would surely swarm her as soon as they realized she'd resurfaced. With luck, that wouldn't happen until she headed home.

We hadn't spoken of how we would break the news of our wedding. Hell, we hadn't spoken much at all, so busy exploring each other. But now it was time to get down to the business of day-to-day living. And in D.C., that meant a lot more than worrying about the mortgage and the car payments.

Once I'd unpacked all but my underwear and stowed my stuff in the closet of a second room (her cupboard and dresser being too small to hold both her garments and mine), I surveyed my new home. Wandering about the mostly empty Georgian, I contemplated the ways I could help Sarah adjust to life in the capital, and how I could make the capital adjust to Sarah.

DETAILS NEEDED ATTENDING. My first order of business: Take the room key back to the hotel and officially check out. The manager glared at me—no doubt the maids had reported the suite empty—but said nothing when I produced a credit card and paid in full. I was not about to let my former employers stiff the hotel or leave Sarah holding the bag (which I suspected they would have done; it might have been part of the enemy's plan).

All went smoothly, my card being in good standing, and I headed out the front door. But, to my displeasure, I ran into Vince on his way in.

"Hey, Mac!" he called, and he jogged over to slap my back. "Where've you been? I heard you disappeared."

My smile likely looked a lot more annoyed than friendly. I said, "I was busy."

He leaned and lowered his voice. "How was she?"

I eyed him without comment a moment. Then, I said, "My business is my business."

He nodded knowingly, "That bad, huh?"

I insisted, "Like I said: no one's business but mine."

"Right," he replied with another nod, but his eyes and tone darkened with irritation. "You always were the gentleman type."

I retorted, "Discretion wins more regulars than gossip, Vince. You oughta try it sometime."

He just grunted and walked away while I quelled the urge to punch his lights out.

I BOUGHT A SECOND-HAND JAG identical to the one I'd rented the other day. (I've always loved the look of a sleek black Jag.) A thorough inspection outside, inside, and under the hood convinced me it was in prime condition, probably just traded for a new model, a different make, or a flashy colour. Unlike some, I didn't care that it was a year old. Better that way: No fake "new car" smell. (I told them the deal was off if they sprayed that crap in it.)

And it purred when I drove it out of the lot and toured the streets of Washington.

After a ride along the Potomac, I turned back to get on with my errands.

MONEY WAS NEXT ON MY LIST. I opened three checking and three savings accounts: a linked pair in each of three different banks. Then, I opened another checking and a safe deposit box in two more. I'd never believed in putting my eggs in one basket, and that had saved my financial ass when I lost half my cash in one of the savings-and-loan scandals. Afterward, I'd made a point of spreading my bread over five institutions instead of two. (There are few things I hate more than being short of funds: I had enough of poverty in my early years in Pittsburgh.)

When I exited the last, a bank on M Street, a glimpse of a woman about Sarah's age reminded me we'd better get a joint checking, too. I could shift a couple of thousand to it once we set it up. Maybe I should put her on one or two of the accounts I'd just opened, I supposed. But I decided to keep those for myself. Who knew how long we'd be together? As the thought ran through my head, my gut seized and, for no apparent reason, I suddenly couldn't get enough air.

EXERCISE WAS WHAT I NEEDED. Yeah, that was all that was wrong with me, I figured as I sucked oxygen all the way to the auto tower. I took the elevator and then sat in the car with my phone out to google local gyms. The city map showed me the locations of those nearest the brownstone, but I wanted to look farther afield. One lay a few blocks away from the bank I'd just left; so, I got out of the car again, locked up, walked down the littered and stinking stairs and out of the multilevel parking structure, and strode on past increasingly modest shops to the rear of an old brick building that bore a faded sign above the painted-metal back door. It read only, "Lou's."

Up I climbed on worn wooden stairs, inhaling with pleasure the smell of years of sweat that permeated the place. Through an open door on the top floor I spotted a grizzled, unshaven, fat, cigar-smoking old-timer and knew at once this must be Lou. His faded jeans and grey sweatshirt blotched with coffee stains made me chuckle to myself. This felt like home already.

He noticed me. He looked me up and down, and his cocked brow and narrowed eyes told me he was not impressed by my immaculate dark silk-wool blend slacks, matching silk shirt, and gleaming patent loafers.

"What brings you here, Sport?" he demanded as I sidestepped a couple of men lifting weights.

When I reached him, I answered, "I'm new in town and looking for a place to work out." I glanced around at the long windows; the rows of equipment by the walls, most weight units and benches in use; and the square platform in the center where a pair of red-faced youngsters no more than twenty grappled beyond the perimeter ropes of the ring under the watchful eye of a middle-aged trainer.

Looking back to Lou, I said, "I like the smell of this place. How much to join up?"

The old man grinned. "Like the smell, huh?" He shook his head and chuckled. Then, he gestured to an open door and led me to his office beyond a half-glazed wall looking out on the gym.

I DIDN'T HAVE TIME to fetch my sweats and go back to Lou's. Besides, I was breathing fine, now. (Must have been a bout of hay fever that set me off, I figured, though I never had that before. Fucking D.C.)

But I needed a shower to wash off the city dust and a bite to eat before I changed to a suit for the evening's activities.

I'd purchased long-stem roses at a florist shop I spied on the way back to the car. In Sarah's kitchen, I filled the vase I'd bought along with the flowers, remembering the woman didn't have a single object not purely practical in function. She didn't have much at all, I'd noticed when I scouted the house. As I arranged the roses in the cut-glass container, I decided that she and I should spend the weekend filling the cupboards. I dismissed the notion of furnishing the place except with a bed comfortably big enough for the two of us because the brownstone was in desperate need of a paint job and new flooring. No sense buying chairs and tables and shelving only to have to move and cover them.

I realized as I stepped into the tub and pulled the plastic curtain that I actually liked the idea of sprucing this place up. I had a few skills picked up in my youth: Mom had insisted I learn several trades so I could pose as a carpenter, a gardener, a mechanic, a pool cleaner—whatever the clients wanted. So all I needed now was an assortment of tools and some paint and varnish. And maybe a ladder and some garden equipment.

I found myself actually looking forward to renovating the house.

Chapter 6

EXPOSURE

IN RED SILK LOUNGING PANTS, I grabbed up the newspaper from the front stoop and then parked myself at the kitchen table, facing the tiny television that perched on a countertop under the side window. The sandwich I'd managed to put together from the few items in the fridge that looked to be a third- or fourth-hand Whirlpool would not sustain me long, but I had plans for dinner.

The bread had to be toasted because she kept it in the freezer compartment. That seemed odd until I realized that a loaf would mold waiting to be consumed by a lone woman who probably ate no more than two slices a day, max. I recalled that she'd preferred salads to sandwiches, back in Vegas. Well, I didn't eat much bread, either.

As I chewed the chicken on organic multigrain, surprised she'd sprung for the good stuff when money was tight, I clicked the remote a few times looking for a weather report. But I stopped at once and jacked up the sound when I glimpsed Sarah surrounded by reporters. My fists tightened as I watched the bastards badger her, not letting her get more than a couple of words out before they tore into her again with biased questions and unsupported innuendo.

My appetite evaporating in an instant, I punched the remote to turn off the squawk-box, tossed the food into the garbage, and stalked up the stairs to change, all the while mulling how best to get those goddamned muckrakers off my wife's back.

I PULLED INTO A SPACE in the visitors' parking lot and turned off the engine. Still steaming, I closed my eyes, took a few deep breaths, and stretched my fingers to relax the hands that had clenched the steering wheel the whole way. As my pulse slowed and my mind cleared, I plucked up the single rose I'd brought from home and exited the car to stride with steely determination to the building that housed the offices of elected representatives.

I knew where she was. I'd been through that particular section of Capitol Hill years ago, in the old days before I decided to avoid the whole Washington scene. I signed in at the entry, casually engaging in brief conversation the guards who scanned for contraband (always a good idea to get friendly with security), before continuing on toward the corridor where I'd seen Sarah buckling under the reporters' assaults.

I rounded a corner and there they were: still hemming her in front of her office and flinging baseless accusations and scurrilous questions.

As I approached, I cleared my throat. Then, I belted out a melody in my best baritone.

"Come to me.
Love me my darling.
You fill my heart with desire
And I long for your touch."

The crowd and cameras focussed on me as I pushed past, my eyes locked with Sarah's.

"Come to me.

*Give me your passion.
I want you, my angel, I need you
And love you so much."*

I ended the song with Sarah in my arm, brushed her face with the rose, and bent her back to kiss her with every ounce of ardour I had. The suit was summer-weight silk, and I'm sure my erection showed when I righted her and smiled into her blushing face.

Someone called out, "Are you her toy boy, McAlister?"

My face turned to stone, I'm sure, as I looked toward the voice and stated through my teeth, "I'm her husband, asshole."

Flashes, as camera shutters blinked.

Staring hard at the man I guessed to be the mouthpiece, I inquired suspiciously, "And how is it you know my name but don't know that?"

He hesitated a moment and I could see his mind churning. Then, he said, "I've seen you around. You're a gigolo."

"Really," I retorted. "I'm new in town. So, exactly when and where did you see me?"

Now he was sweating.

"Last week. Cavorting with society matrons."

"Really," I repeated. "You must need glasses, because I was nowhere near your society matrons—all of whom, I'm sure, would back me up. And I cavorted, as you call it, only with my wife."

"I say I saw you."

"And I say the likes of you make up out of thin air what passes for news these days."

An eager young blonde interjected, "Uh, Mr. McAlister, is it? Sir, how long have you and the Congresswoman been married?"

I noticed she addressed me, not Sarah. I replied, "We married on Thursday and spent a wonderful weekend together before coming home to," I panned the corridor and gestured to the present company, "assaults that purport to be journalism."

Several reporters shifted uncomfortably, including the blonde. Many, not least the mouthy jackass, only glared.

"Now, if you'll excuse us, I'm taking my wife to dinner."

With that, I pulled Sarah toward the exit as reporters scrambled to follow.

THE GREATEST THING ABOUT A JAG is the speed. The second-best is maneuverability. We easily outdistanced the news vans and wove in and out of traffic to slide into the parking lot of the five-star restaurant I'd chosen for tonight's wooing.

But now that I saw Sarah still trembling as we sat to the table in the quiet corner I'd reserved, I knew there would be a lot more comforting than romancing, tonight. Well, it wouldn't be the first time I'd spent an evening calming instead of courting. I clasped and squeezed her hand and held it as I smiled to her. She forced a little smile in return.

A steward placed menus and glasses of water before us. Then, he made himself scarce as I took Sarah's hand in both of mine. I waited for her to suppress the tears that glistened in her eyes and the silent sobs that convulsed her belly. At last, she wiped away the wetness and withdrew her hand to rummage in her purse, produce a hanky, and blow her nose.

"It's always going to be like this, isn't it?"

I assured her, "They've lost their little game, today. They'll kick somebody else for a while."

She said on a breath, "It doesn't help to know someone else will suffer, too." She added, "Especially knowing they'll come back to me eventually."

She whispered, "I never wanted any of this."

I lifted her knuckles to my lips and kissed them. "I know."

I asked, "Do you want to resign and give the job to someone else?"

At that, she inhaled deeply. "No," she answered. "I can't ask the taxpayers to fund another election." She pinched her lips together a moment before she added, "Besides: I'm a citizen. Looking out for our democracy and the people of my state is as much my responsibility as anyone else's."

"Atta girl," I said, smiling proudly. "You'll do better than either of those jerks who wanted the job."

"Why would anybody want it?" she wondered.

"Money," I said. "Kickbacks. Bribes. Offers of very lucrative jobs after they leave office. A chance to play big-shot. The power to make laws that let their company off the hook for taxes or pollution or worker benefits or whatever. The list is long and undistinguished."

"You're right, of course. I wish you weren't."

She sat silent a moment. Then, she whispered, "They'll be back."

I knew what she meant. With a sigh, I said, "Yeah. That's why I think I should go on record and admit who I am. It's only a question of time before somebody furnishes proof of what I do and starts a media feeding frenzy that will hurt you a lot more than it'll hurt me. Better I should put it out in the open myself. Maybe I can spin it in a way that doesn't look bad for you."

She snorted a brief, sad snicker.

I squeezed her hand lightly. Trying to sound confident, I said, "We'll manage." Then, I grinned and added, "And if it all goes south, we'll move to Oregon and start a commune."

She laughed.

Chapter 7

CONFESSIONS

I CHOSE A LOCAL public broadcasting station. After checking out the operation and the PBS reporters for a couple of days, watching their programming and following the crew as they videoed kids playing football, firefighters inspecting a tenement, and a community theatre group rehearsing for a benefit performance, I approached the senior man.

He looked about fifty, maybe fifty-five. His hair had thinned on top and he compensated by cropping all of it short. Tall, about six-two, and sinewy; clean shaven; always dressed in chinos and checked shirts; a well-worn canvas carryall slung over his shoulder; eyes clear and penetrating. And judging by all I'd seen, he was that rare commodity in D.C.: a sensible, honest man who had no interest in running the country for himself.

I waited until he'd finished taping the amateur actors and begun to climb into his van before I strolled over and introduced myself.

"Hi," I said, extending my hand. "I'm Rob McAlister. You don't know me, but I'd like you to interview me for your primetime show."

He glanced to my hand and then to my face before he shook with me firmly and said, "I know the name McAlister. Aren't you the fellah who came out of nowhere and married the Minnesota Congresswoman?"

"Yes."

"And you want me to interview you." He sounded more than a little dubious.

"Yes," I confirmed. "I have something to say, and people are going to want to hear it."

He pursed his mouth thoughtfully and looked me over a moment before he said, "Your place or mine?"

I grinned. "That's usually my line. How

about mine?"

He cocked an eyebrow. "Mary Street, right?"

"Yes. One twenty-five."

"I've got a meeting in the morning. Tomorrow afternoon good for you?"

"I'll be there."

I SPENT MOST OF THE MORNING at Lou's, working off nervous energy and strategizing while I pumped iron. The old man watched me, chewing his unlit cigar, but he didn't ask questions and made no comments.

On the way back to Georgetown, I picked up a few tools from a hardware store. Groceries from a mom-and-pop six blocks from the brownstone finished my errands. Then, I whiled away the remaining hours measuring rooms and guesstimating quantities of paint needed to brighten them.

Jeb Salter and his crew arrived just as I placed the tape back into my new toolbox. I showed them around the empty house, describing the repairs I planned as they filmed on the go. Afterward, Salter and I sat on the steps of the back porch as his crew set up lighting, sound, and video equipment; pegged microphones to our collars; measured ambient light and acoustics; and fussed with Jeb's shirt to the latter's annoyance.

Finally, the interview began.

To the camera, the journalist said, "This is Jeb Salter of PBS-DC speaking with Robert McAlister, recently married to Sarah Wagner, newly elected representative for Minnesota."

He turned to me. "Mr. McAlister, how did you meet the distinguished lady from Minnesota?"

"I was hired to have sex with her."

Salter blinked. I'd told him nothing of what I intended to say and he had certainly not expected so startling and outrageous an answer to what should have been a mildly interesting intro. To his credit, he recovered quickly to ask, "Hired by whom?"

"That's a very good question. I don't know. I got my instructions by text from the escort service I worked for."

"A service here in Washington?"

"No," I told him. "I was based in Miami. I only took the job because the man originally assigned to it asked me to cover the gig while he went into rehab."

"You call it a gig. Is that a common term in your...profession?"

I smiled. "We don't like to call them dates. It's business, not romance."

"Some would see it as combining the two."

"They'd be wrong," I stated with emphasis, no longer smiling. "Yes, some men get into the escort business thinking it's a great way to get laid and get paid at the same time. But they don't last long. To make a successful career, you have to realize it's not about your own pleasure but the client's."

"Even if you don't like the client?"

"Even if you don't like the client."

"Not so easy, then."

"Not always," I affirmed. "Don't get me wrong: There are some gigs that are fun, and some clients who are appealing. But others are just plain hard work." I added, "Just as I'm sure there are some days you enjoy your work and others that you'd rather go fishing."

He laughed. "And some so bad I'd rather be cleaning out a latrine!" He allowed, "But this is definitely not one of those."

I grinned.

"So," he said, "if she didn't hire you, as you implied, Ms. Wagner must have been very surprised at your attentions."

My smile faded. I said quietly, "The text I received claimed the client wanted a rape fantasy."

One of the crewmen swore in a whisper, "Holy shit!"

I went on, "I'd gone to her house and started the game, but it quickly became clear to me that something was wrong. She wasn't responding the way clients who ask for that particular performance do. For a moment there, I wasn't even sure I had the right address. So I asked."

Salter expelled a startled cross between a chuckle and a gasp. "You just asked, 'Are you the woman I'm supposed to rape?'"

"Something like that."

"What did she say?"

"She didn't know what to make of it, at first. And I'd frightened her."

A technician in back murmured too loudly, "No shit!" and Salter darted an irritated glance the woman's way.

I said, "But we discussed it and sorted it out. That is, as best we could, under the circumstances."

Salter summarized, "So...you're telling me a person or persons unknown hired you, without your knowledge or consent, to attack a member of the House of Representatives." He concluded, "That would surely have led to your arrest."

"Yes."

"It appears the escort business is a lot more dangerous than one would imagine."

"It can be."

Salter wondered aloud, "Does Ms. Wagner have any idea who might have done this?"

"No," I said. With a slight smile, I added, "She's an innocent in so many ways. Not at all like me. And a hard worker. She takes her responsibility as a member of Congress seriously."

I could see by his face that Salter wanted to say, "Unlike many of her colleagues." But he kept that to himself and instead observed, "So the two of you married. An unlikely couple."

Before he could probe the reason for our hasty nuptials, I said, "She takes my breath away." And I meant it.

He searched my eyes a long moment. Finally, he remarked, "They do say opposites attract."

"So they do."

He turned the conversation back to my

occupation. "Mr. McAlister, will you be continuing in your career?"

"No," I said. "I left the company. From now on, I'm a one-woman man."

Chapter 8

PROMISES

THE INTERVIEW HAD BEEN EDITED to remove comments from the crew and dead air when no one spoke for a period greater than a second or two. Salter and the station management kindly screened the final result at a private viewing the next evening, prior to the public release. Sitting in the dark, watching me bare my soul on camera, Sarah squeezed my hand. Later, as we walked out to the parking lot, she glanced to me again and again.

"Something on your mind?" I asked as I

opened the door for her.

She started to speak, but changed her mind, shook her head, and slid onto the passenger-side seat. I closed the door and walked around to the driver side, certain she wanted to tell me something and equally certain she would require prodding before she spit it out.

Neither of us spoke on the way to the house, and the silence stretched on as we undressed and prepared for bed.

I leaned against the jamb of the bathroom doorway, watching her brush her teeth. She'd pulled on a cotton gown, a sleeveless nightie in pink-and-white print with ruffled hem and lace-edged neckline. It was the sort of thing you saw on racks in cheap stores and wondered who bought such a hideous design. Strangely, I liked it on her. It *was* her: comfortably feminine, primly practical, old-fashioned and unassuming.

And the fluffy pink slippers added the perfect dash of whimsy. I smiled.

She rinsed the toothbrush and dropped it into its cup. When she turned and saw me grinning, she blushed and bowed her head and tried to pass by. My arm shot out to block her.

"Not yet, Mrs. McAlister," I murmured. I pulled her to me and reached around to press her against the hardness below.

She glanced up and back down with a bashful, breathy giggle.

"I want you," I whispered as I massaged her buttocks. "Damn, but I want you!"

I picked her up and carried her to the bed and made love to her until she protested a need for sleep. Then, I spooned with her, holding her close in the dark, and urged, "Are you ready to tell me, now?"

She remained mute a minute...two minutes.

At last, she said, "It was kind of you to make them think you love me."

I rolled and switched on the bedside light. When I turned back, she still lay curled away and I knew she was afraid to look at me. I grasped her shoulder and pulled her onto her back. Then, I clasped her chin and forced her face out of the shadows, around toward me.

"What do you mean by that, Sarah?"

Her misty eyes darted here and there, looking everywhere but into mine.

"Tell me," I insisted.

She dared a few very brief glances my way before she said, "That part about how I take your breath away."

"Sarah," I whispered. "Sarah, look at me."

When she did as I asked, I declared, "You do, Sarah. You do take my breath away. And I've wanted you from that first night. Wanted you in a way I've never wanted a woman before."

Her face conveyed her fears and doubts.

"I mean it," I insisted. "I will never lie to you. I will never treat you like a client. You're different, Sarah. And when I'm with you, I want to be a different man. A better man."

Tears rolled across her temples and I brushed them away.

To my surprise, she said, "You are a good man."

My expression must have shown my inability to agree.

Turning over to face me squarely, she rose on an elbow and stated firmly, "You *are*. Rob, no one in my life, not even my family, has ever stood up for me before. No one ever tried to protect me the way you've done, again and again, since we met. None of them would have put themselves out the way you have, unless they had something to gain from it." She began to sob as she finished, "No one cared enough."

I pulled her into my arms and rocked her as she wept against my chest. I stared at the ceiling wishing I were the man she thought I was. After what she said, how could I tell her the truth: that I married her as much to save my own skin as to save hers?

She drifted off, but I lay there trying to recall if I'd ever known anyone to truly give a damn about me, and wondering why a sweet woman like Sarah believed no one cared about her.

Chapter 9

NEWS

"HEY, SPORT! YOU'RE ON T.V.!"

I eased the barbells to the rack and jogged over to Lou's office as others gathered there. To my surprise, Jeb Salter had put the interview on the morning show.

The guys glanced to me and back to the television in the far corner a few times, but Lou just grunted and grinned like he'd known all along what I was. He probably had.

I pushed back through the crowd and settled on a bench to press a few with the morning replaying in my mind: I'd driven Sarah to work and given her a long, lazy kiss at the security desk while politicians, bureaucrats, hangers-on, and other flotsam and jetsam flowed around us on their way to one office or another. Then, I walked back to the Jag feeling like a million bucks because I'd seen the new respect on the faces of the denizens of Capitol Hill: Sarah was no longer just a mousy little rookie from Back-of-Beyond; now, she had sex appeal, and that counts even in Congress.

I finished up, showered, and headed home to meet the delivery truck hauling the shitload of paint and the ladder Sarah and I had bought on Saturday. I wanted to get started on those windows. The masonry was in good shape, but peeling paint screamed, "Trash lives here"; so, the exterior was a priority. (The tiled roof would have to be repaired by contractors and I was still looking for a competent firm that wouldn't gouge us.)

The truck pulled up in front a half-hour after I parked in the garage. I'd changed to my "carpenter" jeans and tee, their function now being real work instead of pretence for a gig fantasy, and I caught the lustful look of the woman among the hardware store's personnel as she hauled paint cans up the steps, the load strapped to a rolling hand truck. I smothered a grin.

Once the colours were sorted into the rooms they would decorate and the varnish for the floors was stowed in the basement, I climbed the ladder left out front and began to scrape away old paint. I noticed the vans parked along the street and the news crews aiming cameras at me, but I ignored them to get on with my renovation work. Neither did I pay mind to the plain white van with no markings whatsoever and the Lotus that drove by and parked a few doors down across the way.

Until a beautiful woman in sensually swaying blue silk dress and matching spike heels stepped out of the Lotus and sauntered to the brownstone to stand below.

She was a stranger. No one I'd ever seen, much less worked for. And as she stood there and called up to me, the hairs rose on the back of my neck. I decided not to come down. And I decided we needed a tall fence and a lockable gate for our postage-stamp-sized front yard.

"Who are you and what do you want?" I demanded.

"Darling," she called plenty loud, "don't

tell me you've forgotten our date."

I panned the reporters. They were all aiming mics as well as cameras. I wanted to beat the crap out of every one of them. Her, I just wanted to shove out onto the street. And if she fell on her ass, that was fine with me.

I said as loudly, "I don't know you, and I sure as hell have no intention of knowing you; so, get off my property. You're trespassing."

She smiled and shouted, "But sweetheart, you promised!"

I repeated in full voice (and I can pump the volume to ear-bashing decibels), "Get off my property, bitch! I've never seen you in my life and I don't want to see you ever again. If you're not out of my yard in three seconds, I'll call the cops to haul you away." I pulled out my cell phone.

She pouted prettily and then turned away with a smile and sashayed to the street.

Every muscle in my body tightened as I watched reporters rush forward to interview my fake lover.

My heart pounding, I turned back to scrape with enough force to tear away wood as I tried to figure out how to counter this new attempt to make trouble for Sarah.

Chapter 10

FAKE NEWS

NATURALLY, THE MEDIA SPLASHED narrow images of the strawberry blonde smiling as she strode the brownstone's front walk. Not one shot showed me on the ladder. Instead, somebody had photoshopped me into the frame standing in the doorway, behind her, shirtless in the red silk lounging pants that left little of me to the imagination. All the mainstream ran it. (How do these guys live with themselves?) And the woman lied through her teeth in the phony interview, claiming we'd "known each other" for years—which she emphasized in a way that left no doubt she meant in the biblical sense.

Sarah didn't say a word when I picked her up that evening, but I could tell she'd seen the vids. And everybody we passed either glared at me with disapproval or grinned with sardonic glee. I made a point of memorizing the faces of the latter.

In the driver's seat of the Jag, the key in the ignition but not yet engaged, I turned to her and stated emphatically, "It's all a put-up job, Sarah. I don't know that woman from Eve."

When she sat still, downcast, and said nothing, my heart and gut competed for space at my knees.

Desperate, I said, "I promised you I'll never lie to you, Sarah, and I won't. I'm not lying. She's a stranger to me, and she just walked up while I was working outside and pretended we had an appointment."

"I know."

I blinked and swallowed, not sure whether she meant that or just wanted to end the conversation.

She looked up at me then. "Those pants are in the laundry basket, and I know who she is."

I took that in. Yes, I'd tossed them into the hamper; hadn't thought of that. But if she knew the woman....

"Is she the one you told me about? The one who filed papers for the election?"

"No," she said with a touch of steel in her tone. "But I have no doubt she put Marianne up to it." She looked to me again. "Marianne Martin is notorious in Minneapolis. She's had three husbands—all rich—and they all divorced her for sleeping around. So she has no reputation to lose by playing the slut." She snorted a bitter laugh. "In fact, she'll probably snare herself another rich husband while she's here. One more interested in her body than her morals."

"Plenty of those in town," I replied. My belly eased as I realized she really did believe me. And a voice in my head wondered why that mattered so much. I started the car.

"Let's just go home," I said. "I'll make a fabulous supper."

"You don't have to."

"Yes, I do," I insisted. "I'll feed you and give you a massage and make you forget all about this."

She smiled then, that shy little smile that always made my heart sing. And I drove home as fast as the traffic would allow.

SHOULD HAVE KNOWN the newshounds would be waiting there. They blocked the garage.

"Stay here," I said on a disgusted sigh. "I'll clear the way."

But Sarah climbed out of the car as I did, and she marched to the nearest crew, grabbed the mic from the blathering newsy who was trying to question her, and said vehemently and straight into the camera, "Did you think I wouldn't recognize her, Lauren? Did you really think I'd let you take my husband from me?"

With that, she shoved the mic back at the reporter, pushed past the dumbfounded media morons, stalked to the gate, unlocked it, and slammed it behind her as she strode on to the house.

I didn't know she had it in her.

After a moment of shocked silence, someone asked, "McAlister, who's Lauren?"

Shrugging shoulders and eyebrows, I said, "Beats the hell out o' me." Then I glared to them all and growled, "Now, get the hell out of my way or I'll run you over."

"We can sue!" yelled some smartass.

I retorted, "Not if I back over you a few times to make sure."

I pressed the remote on my key ring and the crews grudgingly moved out of the way. When I drove in, I closed the door behind me before I exited the car. Maybe they thought I'd deck them, or maybe they were afraid I'd press charges of trespassing, but none tried to duck inside. As I hurried to the house, I decided I'd better find out who Lauren was.

I PUSHED A FEW STRANDS of hair from her rosy face and smiled into her glassy eyes. Damn! but Sarah was fine when she looked at me like that: sated and happy and trusting. I could fall into her eyes and live there forever.

I suddenly wondered: Is this what love is? Is this how it feels?

I huffed a laugh, then, and I looked away, self-conscious.

"What is it?" Sarah asked, her smile fading as her anxiety flared.

I chewed my lip a moment before I dared to reply. Feeling bashful for the first time since I-don't-know-when and not certain she'd believe me, I murmured, "I think I love you."

She just lay there staring at me, searching my face for what felt like hours. Then, she caressed my cheek and whispered, "I love you, too."

My heart could have filled the room.

Chapter 11

A'HUNTING

SARAH'S CHALLENGE to the unknown woman never made it to the airwaves, the presses, or to cyberspace. *Quelle surprise.* (Yeah, I'd learned a little French along the way.)

But Terry called to tell me he'd seen my interview on the Miami PBS station, and Salter said it was being aired here and there throughout the country.

I DIDN'T KNOW A SOUL in Minneapolis. Nor did Terry. And I didn't trust any of my old colleagues or acquaintances to help me out. I had no idea how I would track down this Lauren woman. So I was distracted when I yanked on my sweats and then picked up a barbell at Lou's. I must have looked fierce, because nobody spoke a word to me until the old-timer planted himself in front of me and said, "You keep that up and you won't have enough strength to lift a bar of soap."

At his comment, I realized my arm was shaking. "Thanks," I said, and I switched to the other arm to add equal muscle mass to that side.

"Come see me when you're done," Lou commanded.

I looked at him and nodded.

A while later, showered and changed and both arms feeling like spaghetti, I walked into Lou's office and asked, "What's up?"

He said, "That's my line."

I mulled a moment, considering whether to tell him. But I decided to trust him; he had a way about him that inspired confidence. So I closed the door and sat in the lone wooden guest chair across the desk perpetually strewn with piles of paper that might have been arranged in a kind of filing system. Lou leaned back.

"Talk to me."

I took a deep breath. Then, despite having

met this man a mere week ago and knowing nothing of him save his brand of cigars, I laid out the whole situation as I knew it.

When I finished, he stared at me a minute or two with his mouth pushed out and his mashed stogy in his right hand. Then, he clamped the cigar between his teeth and started searching his desk. He said, "Got a friend in Minneapolis might be able to find out who this broad is."

"Thanks," I said with my brows high in surprise. I'd figured to get my troubles off my chest, but I hadn't figured the man could help.

"Here it is," Lou announced as he pulled a scrap of paper from under one of the piles. He handed it to me. "He's a shamus. Retired, officially. But I know he could use the cash and he has all the time in the world to track this Lauren down."

I took the note and read the name and number. I wondered, "How do you know him?" I really meant, "Can I trust him?" But Lou knew that.

"Old Army buddy. He's a straight shooter. Wouldn't stiff ya."

I looked up to Lou and nodded. "Okay. Thanks. I'll give him a call."

"You do that."

As I stood up, he added, "Go get 'er, Sport. We don't want any more trouble for your lady, there."

"No, we don't."

INSTEAD OF WALKING DOWN, I marched up to the roof and checked the indicator on my cell to be sure of my reception. All bars glowed. So I punched in the number on my pad and hit the connect button.

As the rings registered at my ear, I paced and glanced about at the other rooftops and the taller towers visible from here. I didn't know whether any reporters were waiting downstairs, but I didn't want to take a chance. And I was pretty sure one of the new guys at the gym was a journo looking to catch me unawares to get a scoop; he asked too many questions.

Up here, I was alone. Nobody could record my conversation, at least not without my knowing it. Well, except maybe the N.S.A. And I figured they wouldn't take interest in a small fry like me.

"Barker."

I chuckled that the name fit the sound. I told him, "Lou Cassidy gave me your number. My name's McAlister."

"Wouldn't be Rob McAlister, would it?"

I grinned to myself. Sharp, this one. "Yeah. That's me. And I want to commission you to find out all you can about a woman named Lauren Hartwell, friend of Marianne Martin."

"I know Martin well enough. Tracked her for her first husband before their divorce. And Hartwell—that's her maiden name, by the way, daughter of the senator—is a well-known socialite."

"I want to know why the senator's daughter has it in for my wife." I added, "And what I can do about it."

"How bad you want to know?"

My mouth pulled awry. Yeah. A sharp one. Even retired, he would not come cheap.

Chapter 12

WAITING GAME

I KNEW IT WOULD TAKE TIME. A senator's daughter wouldn't leave her secrets lying about like so much carelessly discarded lingerie. Mommy and Daddy would have taught her to keep the soiled linen well hidden. So there was nothing to do but wait and hope Barker could turn up something useful. Something dirty enough to keep the bitch at bay.

It struck me as odd that the offspring of a wealthy politician would even know much less take an active dislike to the daughter of an unemployed labourer and a waitress. The two girls would have lived on opposite sides of the tracks, going to different schools and belonging to social circles so far apart they might as well have been on separate planets. Certainly, if they were to cross paths and the rich kid did decide to toy with the poor kid, the former would have the means to cause trouble for the latter.

But why? And was Senator Hartwell aware of his daughter's cruel games?

I'd seen Hartwell up close, once, at a party in Miami, and judged him a typical D.C. dickhead. His wife seemed the longsuffering type who tolerated the political life and the people her husband cultivated for the sake of votes. No doubt tolerated his affairs, as well, and drank to numb the anger. Growing up in a family like that, children would likely come to consider themselves entitled to do as they pleased. And the parents would either fail to notice their kids' antics, too busy with their ambitions and social calendar, or would cover them up to prevent scandal in public and emotional scenes at home.

I was thinking along these lines while I drove Sarah to Rock Creek Park for a day away from reporters, House speeches, and looky-loos.

With the car parked and the picnic basket in hand, I linked arms with my wife and we strolled along to the river, enjoying dappled sunshine, the twitters of birds, babbling waters, and wafting breezes as the temperatures soared above a hundred.

"Why do you think this Lauren hates you?" I asked without preamble.

"I don't know," Sarah answered. "I don't remember meeting her before she came up to me in the schoolyard, one day, and started calling me names. Saying I was trash who'd come from trash and I'd grow up to be a slut like my mother."

I frowned. "In the schoolyard? Did she go to the same school?"

"No. I thought maybe she did, at first. But she wore a uniform, and one of my classmates recognized the crest as belonging to a private school on the edge of town. Nevertheless, Lauren started coming by with friends to taunt me every few weeks. And she'd show up at school events or in my neighbourhood to make trouble. Later on, she even cost me jobs, making complaints and getting me fired."

She heaved a sigh. "I wanted to leave town and get as far from her as I could."

With a world-weary smile, Sarah looked

up to me and added, "I scrimped and saved for it, only to end up here, broke, and still being her whipping-girl."

I stopped, set down the picnic basket, and tossed the blanket Sarah had been carrying on top. Then, I cupped her face and bent to kiss her. When I straightened, I said, "We're not broke. And, one way or another, we'll get her off your back."

Sarah reached her arms around me and clung as I held her under the shade of a sycamore. Sometime later, we spread the blanket and enjoyed potato salad, mixed-vegetable vinaigrette, cold beef, and a smooth California red. We topped it off with sharp cheddar and green grapes before Sarah hiked to the public washroom to heed a nature call. The rest of the afternoon, we just sat on the grass and watched the water flow on its way to the bay and the ocean beyond.

I marvelled that we didn't need to talk. Just being together was enough.

INVITATIONS FLOODED IN. Sarah balked, at first, afraid she had nothing appropriate to wear to a Washington shindig. She was right. So I took her shopping.

The price tags in the first three boutiques

sent her running for the exit. When I realized she would never agree to a designer dress that cost more than her year's salary as a waitress, I scouted for second-hand stores and consignment shops where she might find something with class that didn't require selling off of body parts. The moment I stepped into *The Vintage Rose,* I knew I'd found the right place.

A week later, Sarah and I walked arm in arm into a mansion styled on the classical Greek school, I in white dinner jacket with black tuxedo slacks and cummerbund, she in nineteen-twenties gown of beaded black silk, black faux-pearl teardrop earrings skimming her neck, her upswept hair held by Spanish combs. She looked smashing, and I couldn't have been more proud.

The butler led us to the ballroom where guests dripping with diamonds had already gathered, and the hostess greeted us effusively.

"My dear Mr. and Mrs. McAlister," gushed Mrs. Nora Clift, wife of senior Senator George Clift, "I am so pleased you could join us. You know Mr. David Sullivan and his wife, Congresswoman Debra Bromley Sullivan?"

"Of course," Sarah replied as she extended her hand. The Sullivans each shook with us, and the evening got off to a friendly start.

But the pleasantries didn't last long.

I noticed Vince, first, beyond a clutch of women, he standing by the buffet tended by white-suited waiters. When the gaggle of matrons moved off to greet newcomers, I saw the woman Vince escorted: Kimberly Griffiths. The bleached blonde with Florida tan spotted me and immediately dragged her new gigolo across the room, all but running to confront Sarah and me.

"Rob, darling," she cooed. "How wonderful to see you again."

"Hello, Kimberly," I said without enthusiasm. I asked pointedly, "Have you met my wife, Sarah?"

Sarah held out her hand, but Kimberly only brushed her aside to slip her arm into mine while Vince grabbed Sarah's hand and started to pull her away. Sarah resisted, and Vince tugged the harder as Kimberly tried to steer me to the dance floor.

Sarah's frightened eyes spurred me to wrench free of the socialite and stalk to Vince to clamp his wrist and dig my fingers into his flesh. "Get your hands off my wife," I hissed low, my eyes promising retribution if he refused.

"Rob, dear," Kimberly persisted, trying to pull me away, her voice rising, "Vince can entertain Sally."

My eyes remained locked with Vince's. He knew me: We'd had a run-in before, when he got rough with the wrong woman at a soirée in Tampa and I cleaned his clock; so, after a couple of seconds, he relented and let go of Sarah. She trembled visibly as she stepped back.

"Rob, don't be a bore. Dance with me," Kimberly demanded, yanking my arm insistently. The room had quieted as everyone watched the little drama unfolding before them.

Pulling out of the blonde's grasp, I snarled, "I don't take orders, Mrs. Griffiths. And if you want action, that's what you pay Vince for."

As the woman gaped, I whirled and put my arm around Sarah to usher her out the door. I brought her to the vestibule before I stopped and hugged her. "I'm sorry," I whispered. "I didn't expect to see anybody I knew, here. But I guess this sort of thing will just keep happening." I admitted, "My past will always get in the way."

Mrs. Clift caught up with us. "Oh, my dears, I do hope you'll stay and enjoy the party."

I might have thought our hostess genuinely desired our company did I not spy a crafty gleam in her eye. She'd set us up, I was sure.

"Thanks for the offer," I said, "but I'll be

taking my wife home, now."

Ignoring the woman's protests, I drew Sarah outside and then lifted her into my arms to carry her to the Jag.

MASCARA TRAILED BLACK LINES down her cheeks. I stepped up behind and wrapped my arms around her to rock with her as we stared into the bathroom mirror.

"I'll never fit in here," she whispered.

"That makes two of us," I said.

She sighed. "But I can't just leave."

I suggested, "Sure you can. I still have plenty of cash. We could pull up stakes and settle somewhere else. Kansas, maybe. Or Oklahoma. Get a small spread and raise some chickens."

She emitted a little chuckle. "I can't picture you as a farmer."

"Neither can I. But I'd do it for you."

Our eyes met in the mirror and hers welled.

"You're making me cry again." She half-chuckled as she said it.

I pulled the combs from her hair to release her tresses and I kissed her crown.

"I'd rather make you smile."

AUGUST GAVE WAY TO SEPTEMBER and September to October. We tossed social invitations into the recycling bin and stayed home. While I painted walls and repaired trim and oiled squeaky hinges, Sarah studied briefs and bills with the help of a Black's Law Dictionary I'd found in an independent bookstore a block from Lou's. Occasionally, she read documents aloud and we discussed their terms and ramifications. I taught her to look at every piece of legislation with an eye to how it could be misused. And she taught me to imagine a world where it never would.

Chapter 13

SCANDAL

CHRISTMAS HAD COME AND GONE and a storm had blanketed Washington with a half-foot of snow. Abandoned vehicles clogged the Beltway, the Parkway, and the Freeway, and snowplows brought in from northern states gradually cleared highways and interstates as best they could despite the congestion. Another reason to hate D.C.

I left my Jag in the garage, and Sarah and I took cabs wherever we needed to go. Which suited me fine, because I rarely left the warmth of the house except to pick up groceries and to work out at Lou's. I'd been living in the sunny south a long time.

It was a Monday, and Sarah had been called to a special meeting with the Speaker. After seeing her to the Hill, I rode to the gym and changed to my sweats. I worked myself hard, because I hadn't done much but power-sand and varnish floors for the last couple of weeks and I was feeling out of shape. When I finally finished my routine, Lou beckoned me to his office.

"Got a call for you," he said. He handed me a note. "Meet him there."

I glanced to the paper and then to Lou. "Barker?"

"Yup. He's in town."

Finally! I thought. All these months of forking over were about to pay off. I nodded to Lou and hurried to shower and don my woollies and parka. The meeting-place was a good six blocks away.

THE HOTEL WAS A DIVE, but it was warm. I climbed the stairs to the third floor, ignoring the refuse and the smell of vomit and hoping I wouldn't catch fleas or worse. Halfway along the murky corridor lit by two of the five light fixtures, I knocked on the door marked "33."

To my surprise, it opened to a bright-eyed man with salt-and-pepper hair, a trim moustache, and a brown turtleneck that covered a barrel chest. He looked neat and downright dapper in his pressed slacks. Not at all like the hotel's usual clientele. And not much like his pot-bellied friend Lou.

"Barker, I presume."

"You presume correctly," he said as he stepped back to let me into the room furnished with a double bed, a single nightstand, and a wooden chair. The overhead washed the dingy space with golden light, and an open closet on the right abutted an open door that revealed the sink of the small bathroom.

A file folder lay on the bedspread, and Barker waved me to the chair as he sat on the mattress.

"I wasn't dragging my heels," he declared. "What I found was buried deep and some of the witnesses were long dead. But I managed to unearth something very interesting."

He grabbed up the manila folder and handed it to me. My gut tight and my hands shaking with the excitement, I pressed it open to read the top page. My eyes must have been round as saucers when I looked up to the grinning gumshoe.

BARKER HAD MADE me extra copies and I gave one to Lou to hide in his office. Then, I stashed one in each of my safe deposit boxes after making three more on the copy machine of a drugstore. One of those I handed to Salter with a request to sit on it until I gave the okay; one I parked with the lawyer Lou had recommended a while back; and the last I carried to Mary Street and placed in a black-leather Longchamps briefcase I'd bought years ago to keep in my trunk for the women who liked the frisky-boss game. (It was still there, in the Jag. Some habits die hard.)

It was dark by the time I got home. In the kitchen, I switched on the television, about to start preparing supper, and saw Sarah's distressed face. The bastards were hounding her again. But I didn't get the chance to act on my impulse to hop into my car and ride to her rescue because the doorbell rang. The moment I opened it, I knew something was wrong: There stood a pair of burly cops.

"Robert McAlister," said the older one, "you are under arrest for the rape of Annabelle Porter."

I didn't say a word as they cuffed me and

read me my Miranda rights while cameras filmed it all. My mind was awhirl, trying to recall somebody named Annabelle and wondering when I was supposed to have committed this crime.

The trip to the precinct house was uncomfortable, as always. Only a midget would be able to sit normally in the back of a cruiser built with leg space so tight even an average person has to sit sideways, much less anyone with legs as long as mine. Worse, I was shivering because the sonsobitches hadn't let me put on my coat. And, locked in cuffs, I couldn't reach my cell phone to call the lawyer.

I kept my mouth shut while they booked me, still trying to figure out how this had happened. They photographed and printed me. They took my cell, my belt, and my wallet (my keys were still on the kitchen table). Then, they shoved me into a small interrogation room bare of all but a table and a few chairs and they left me to sweat awhile.

When a short and heavyset detective in a rumpled suit finally strode in with his tall and thin partner, the pair laid into me in the usual "we know everything" act. I didn't bother to ask for a lawyer. I just stared at them while they tried to bait me. Sooner or later, I knew, they'd have to let me make my call.

"You've got a long list of priors, McAlister," said the portly one. "Miami, Tampa, New York, Los Angeles, Chicago, New Orleans, and now D.C. Tell me: Is there any town where you haven't abused women?"

I knew he was full of it. Every one of those charges had been dropped when the agency provided proof the client had requested rough treatment, and that would be on file. I also knew that the Miami police, in particular, would vouch for me.

But this was D.C., and nobody here really knew me. Worse, somebody with clout was out to get me.

Tiny and Titan hammered away at me for well over three hours before the lawyer arrived. As soon as he presented his credentials, the two stopped browbeating me and waited while young Lawrence Utronki of Utronki and Paroschy questioned me about my treatment at the hands of the police force.

"They've been spouting bullshit and they know it," I told the blond in a grey wool coat that hung open to reveal a navy muffler, charcoal suit, white shirt, and blue tie. "Trying to get me to confess to something I didn't do." I added, "And they drove me here in an unheated cruiser without letting me put on my parka before they cuffed me."

At that, Utronki glared at the detectives, who cast an irritated glance to the silvered window that, no doubt, hid the arresting officers. They were looking at a possible lawsuit if I caught so much as a sniffle.

Then, to my surprise, the lawyer opened his briefcase and handed the cops a file. "You will release Mr. McAlister at once. Witnesses have come forward to verify that my client was nowhere near Ms. Porter on the night in question."

Titan sneered, "I'm sure the Congresswoman would claim she was with her husband."

Utronki retorted, "The Congresswoman doesn't need to claim anything." He pointed to a list on the top sheet that Tiny was reading. "As you can see, she has not been named as a witness." He added, "And Mr. Chisholm called to volunteer his testimony after seeing a news broadcast. One that was aired prematurely, I might add."

I wondered who Chisholm was.

Vowing legal repercussions, the lawyer

escorted me out of the station wrapped in the jacket of a cop my size, and a cruiser followed us to Mary Street to ensure the return of the patrolman's coat.

Reporters mobbed us, of course, but Utronki shouted, "Rest assured that these false charges against Mr. McAlister will be met with counter-charges of our own."

With that, the two of us shouldered our way through the throng and climbed the steps to the doorway where Sarah waited anxiously as flashes brightened the brownstone and paparazzi shouted prejudicial questions. She hugged me a moment before she stepped back to allow us to enter, and I tossed the jacket to the waiting policeman before I closed the door.

Chapter 14

REVELATIONS

THIS WAS D.C. AND NO ONE LET IT DROP. Ms. Annabelle Porter, a woman I'd never seen until I caught a glimpse of her on T.V., regularly and tearfully proclaimed her victimhood to eager newshounds. The D.A. insisted I was still under investigation and insinuated that the "alleged" witnesses had been coerced. And Sarah daily pushed past reporters who spouted innuendo and outright lies.

Barker, I'd learned, had found most of the witnesses. He'd charged into action the moment he saw the televised arrest. And he'd contacted Lou, who called Utronki. This was going to cost me big-time, I knew, but I asked the private eye to see if he could find out who the hell Annabelle Porter was. We already had a fair idea who had hired her.

Weeks passed, with the same old song playing every day on the news as though repetition turned lies into truth. The police refused to name any who had come forward on my behalf, thanks to the ongoing threat of a lawsuit now that I'd developed bronchitis. Nonetheless, the media somehow got hold of the cab driver's name. But all he ever told pestering reporters was, "Fuck you." To his credit, the man's boss gave him time off, and the cabbie took a vacation to parts unknown.

Terry called me daily for moral support; Barker gave me weekly updates; and Lou turfed from his establishment the stringer who tried too forcefully to get a story out of me. Otherwise, I kept to my usual habits, determined not to let it all get to me.

Finally, the break came.

LARRY UTRONKI AND ED BARKER sat at the kitchen table as Sarah and I looked over the file Barker had provided.

"I can't say I'm surprised," Sarah said when she finished reading the evidence that Annabelle Porter and Lauren Hartwell belonged to the same sorority. "But this doesn't prove Annabelle's lying. And I still don't understand why Lauren hates me so much."

She turned baffled and anxious eyes to me, and I squirmed. I'd held back the information Barker had given me. But now I could no longer put off revealing the truth. With a grimace to the detective and lawyer, I fetched my briefcase and handed my wife the file that would rock her world.

I'D NEVER SEEN SARAH LIKE THIS: hard-eyed and seething under a calm exterior. There was sadness beneath the anger, I knew, but it would not surface today. Staid in a navy nineteen-fifties Chanel suit she'd found in *The Vintage Rose*, she waited at the lectern as Barker, Lou, Utronki, and I looked on and as reporters set up for the press conference none of them had anticipated. In the spacious room she'd booked for the occasion, Sarah looked over the notes before her. Then, as the room quieted and she panned her audience, she gripped the sides of the tall, narrow reading-desk so tightly her knuckles blanched.

She cleared her throat, leaned to the

microphone, and began.

"I am here to counter the patently false accusations against my husband."

Immediately, someone piped up, "Of course, you'd defend your gigolo—"

"Shut up!" she shouted. "Shut up and listen, you filthy, lying, conniving, toadying pigs!"

You could have heard a mouse creep over the carpet.

"Annabelle Porter is lying. And I have reason to believe she has been put up to it by her sorority sister, Lauren Hartwell Donahue."

Several reporters opened their mouths, but she cut them off.

"You heard me right: The daughter of Senator Paul Hartwell has been making my life miserable in any way she can since she learned that I am her half sister."

Breaths caught. Cameras rolled.

"Two days ago, I discovered that I am the illegitimate daughter of Senator Hartwell. My mother died in childbirth, and the senator paid a down-and-out couple to raise me as their own. I do not know how Lauren became aware she had a sister, but she subsequently went out of her way to bully me and has done so for all the years since—even ensuring I lost a scholarship, a fiancé, and several jobs. And now, she's trying to take my husband from me and have me sent home to Minnesota in disgrace."

"Where's your proof?" a grey-hair in the front row demanded.

At that, she raised a hand, and the boys Lou had brought along stepped away from the walls where they'd been waiting to pick up the files at their feet and distribute them to the reporters. Mutters rose and papers shuffled as the gathered newsmen and women riffled through the documentation.

From the doorway, a loud, rhythmic clapping drew everyone's attention. I recognized the Texan I'd seen months ago as he sauntered into the room and waded through the crowd in his white Stetson, light-grey silk suit, piped Western shirt, black string tie, and tooled cowboy boots. He planted himself next to Sarah and waited, ignoring questions until the reporters fell silent.

At last, Calvin Chisolm drawled, "Y'all know me. God knows I come up here often enough. And I'm here now to tell you I saw this man," he pointed to me, "on the night Jake Porter's daughter claims she was accosted by him. There's no way in hell he could have come all the way across town from the hotel where she says he attacked her, and at the hour she says he attacked her, to have gotten to the room two doors from mine in time for me to spot him. And if she were my daughter, I'd tan her hide for such lies."

With that, he nodded to me, tipped his hat to Sarah, and stalked out with an air of finality, once more ignoring the press.

Closing her file folder, Sarah glared at the journalists before her and declared, "You had better tell this story and tell it truthfully, or I assure you I'll sue every last one of you along with your editors and the owners of your companies."

Head high, she looked like a queen as she strode out of the conference room. I watched after her with my heart bursting.

Chapter 15

KARMA'S A BITCH

THE INVITATIONS that had dwindled to zero began to flood in once more when the shocking tale of sibling rivalry and a senator's infidelity went viral. So many copies of the evidence circulated that a cover-up had become impossible.

Mrs. Joan Hartwell filed for divorce. An official sorority judgment expelled both Annabelle Porter and Lauren Hartwell Donohue. Johnny Smith, a.k.a. Vince DiFlorio (his trade name), and the entire management of the escort service came under investigation and soon found themselves facing conspiracy charges alongside Lauren, several of her cronies, three Congressional aides, and the hotel security man who had been paid to back Annabelle Porter's story.

Another truth surfaced when a clerk remembered that the woman in fine suit, silk scarf, and dark glasses who had registered as a candidate in the by-election looked a lot more like tall and willowy Lauren Hartwell than short and buxom Sarah Wagner. When Sarah confirmed that she had not actually run for office, a Congressional committee decided (despite protests from a few Washington insiders, all connected to Hartwell) that her election would stand for the time remaining of her term.

She assured the members and the electorate that she would not seek office in the coming year.

WE ROLLED DOWN THE WINDOWS of the Jag as we pulled out of the motel parking lot and cruised toward the I-30 to Dallas. We'd engaged a small transport driven by one of Lou's young friends to move our few furnishings separately while we drove on ahead to scout the properties listed for sale in Blue Rock and Pritchard. With luck, we'd own a piece of Texas by the time the truck arrived.

Barker's investigations had much depleted my savings. And the later legal costs when Paul Hartwell tried to defend himself and his daughter—his legitimate daughter—by suing Sarah and me had further drained my...our reserves.

Fortunately, the judge awarded us court costs when the senator lost his case. It also helped greatly that Sarah's pay and benefits as a member of Congress had finally kicked in after a whistleblower's e-mail started an investigation into the delays she'd been experiencing. Again, the problems led back to the Hartwell family. And the brownstone sold for a small profit, thanks to all the work Sarah and I had put into renovating it. (Most of it was my doing, but she did choose the authentic period paint colours and design the garden that clinched the sale.)

Now, her term up and with a modest nest egg at our disposal, we turned our backs to both Washington and Minneapolis and headed for the Lone Star State.

Why had we chosen Texas? Well, aside from the southern weather, we had a friend there: Cattle baron Cal Chisolm offered me a job selling his wife's line of high-end Western wear.

He figured any man who could convince jaded socialites that he was head over heels for them could sell bikinis to Eskimos. (Lana Chisolm recently called to tell us her friends were all atwitter at the prospect of a notorious gigolo in their midst.)

And if ladies' wear didn't work out, the ranch always had room for a man good with his hands.

I'd been happily contemplating a whole new start in life when, out of the blue, Sarah said, "We can skip the place thirty miles outside Pritchard. It won't be big enough."

I frowned. "It's got nearly two hundred acres. That's plenty big, sweetheart."

Sara grimaced a moment before she insisted, "The house is too small."

Something about the way she said it told me we needed to discuss this. I pulled off the road, turned off the engine, twisted in my seat, and demanded, "What do you mean, too small? It's got a kitchen, a living room, a bathroom, a laundry, and a bedroom. What more do we need?"

She wrinkled her nose and smiled guiltily.

"An extra bedroom? Maybe two?"

I blinked. I was about to ask why we

needed the extra rooms when I noticed the way her hand rested on her belly. Then, I noticed how round it had become. I looked into her glowing face and blinked again.

A dad? Me?

I woke up slumped in the driver seat with my little wife tapping my cheek and anxiously calling my name.

CYBER PRINCE CHARMING

CHAPTER 1

Lonely seas

I GRIMACED AND GROANED as I came to muddled consciousness noticing the pain in my head and throat, in particular, and in my body generally. Squinting, I peered up into darkness and wondered how on earth I had come to feel as though I had been tumble-dried for a couple of hours. And what was that putrid stench?

The enveloping black masked my surroundings, but there was no mistaking the solid, cold concrete on which I lay. How did I get here? Where was I?

Something skittered over me on four multi-fingered feet. Instantly, full focus activated my brain and propelled me to a sitting position. Or it would have, had lightning not struck behind my eyes. I collapsed back supine, desperately sucking what air that murky, fetid place afforded me.

As the pain settled to a pounding throb and I lay exhausted by the agony, I searched my memory in hope of recalling what had happened to put me in this predicament. My mind hopped desultorily among images and snatches of conversation.

At a realization, terror knifed through me.

🖳

"BE CAREFUL WHAT YOU WISH FOR," Mom used to say. That, and, "You have the worst luck with men, Connie."

Don't you hate it when your mom's always right?

🖳

FROM CHILDHOOD, I wished for a dream prince. I got Gerry, the first time. He's still my best friend, by the way. But we married in our late teens because we had always been friends since we were about two years old, and everybody said we made the perfect couple. Maybe if we'd slept together beforehand, we'd have realized we weren't meant to be more than best buddies.

Not that we didn't try to make it work, but there was just no spark in the bedroom. When about a year after the wedding Gerry found his true soulmate, I didn't have the heart to deny him his happiness with Brenda.

Then came Dave, apparent answer to my own dream. But his eyes weren't only for me (nor his other parts, for that matter) and that brief marriage ended a lot less amicably.

Tom, my Johnny Cash clone, was more interested in his career and his groupies than in me. He certainly had no desire to marry.

And married or not, Jean-Guy was determined to live down to the well-known reputation of French men.

So after the fourth go (I am a little slow on the uptake), I finally decided to put my wish for a handsome fairytale prince—or at least a faithful husband—on the back burner.

I should have tossed it into the trash along with Jean-Guy's jeans and shoes.

💻

I HAD BEEN WORKING for the trucking company for over two years. It wasn't a great job, but there was little to choose from in my home town. Ordering supplies, keeping track of who was driving which rig, and scheduling shipments for customers beat running my butt off at the diner or standing all day slicing meat at the deli counter of the grocery store (both of which I had tried in my teens). And the pay at Donnegan's Cartage was a little better than minimum wage and came with medical and dental.

There was always down time in the office during winter months because people and businesses tended to wait until spring if they wanted to move to a new location. Sure, companies continued to send goods to clients, many of them across the border, but frantic activity started around the middle of April and continued into mid December, ending with the Christmas rush.

But like I said, things slowed once the snows flew in earnest. After New Year's, cleaning the office and the washroom, counting inventory, and shredding old files once the accountant decided they were no longer needed kept me busy for a while. But by February I was bored out of my mind. I brought hand-quilting projects to work a couple of times, but stopped when my boss Tom knocked my half-finished white-and-blue table runner on the floor where drivers and customers had tracked in filthy snow. I could have killed him, but I swore mostly at myself for bringing it from home in the first place.

After that, I tried novels. But I kept getting dirty looks from several of the guys who, I suspect, could barely read and certainly didn't approve of any books with titles like "Forever Love" or "The Daring Duke." For weeks I ignored their glares and jibes. But when a customer made a wisecrack about finding me reading when he came in, Tom politely suggested I think of something else to do. (That same client had had no problem with my quilting the month before. I can only guess that he, like so many other Neanderthals I know, prefers women ignorant, barefoot, and in the kitchen.)

"Try to look busy," Tom told me.

So, I turned to the internet on my computer when my paperwork was finished and the phones were quiet. Once I tired of reading news and of lifestyle sites and general surfing, I logged into social to read posts by family and friends and, if anyone was available, chatted online through direct messaging.

That's how it all started.

ON A FRIDAY, just after lunch, I filed the last of the waybills, expense vouchers, and Customs forms. There was a blizzard raging outside and many roads were closed; so, scheduled shipments had been put on hold and my inbox was empty. Drivers without loads had been sent home once their trucks had been cleaned, and the mechanics had already knocked off to escape before the squall hit. Since Tom was in bed with flu in his upstairs apartment, and since I lived within walking distance, I stayed to man the phones in case the drivers who were still on the road called in an emergency.

Wishing I'd brought a book after all, I did a quick sweep of the floor, scrubbed the toilet, and finally sat down to stare at my computer screen. I couldn't think of a thing I wanted to look up, and the news just depressed me; so, I clicked on my favourite social site and entered my username and password. As always, there were unread messages; so I checked who had contacted me. To my surprise, there was an invitation from a stranger.

«*Hello. I would like to speak with you.*»

I laughed at first (snorted, really) and frowned and blinked at the simple request from out of the blue. Naturally, I clicked on the guy's image and checked out his page. (I knew better than to just "follow" without digging a little.) His photo and bio and recent posts flabbergasted me: Apparently, he was an honest-to-God prince! Okay, he was a foreign prince living halfway around the world. But he was handsome and rich and...why would somebody like him be the least bit interested in talking to me?

I studied his page: all the events he attended, all the photo ops with celebrities and bigwigs, all the shots and vids of him riding, flying, dancing....

The more I learned of him, the more I wondered if he had maybe hit a wrong button and got me instead of somebody he actually wanted to talk to.

But he sent another message, and I decided it would only be polite to respond.

Hello. Perhaps you have mistaken me for someone else.

«*I assure you, no. I have seen your profile and I became intrigued.*»

I sat a minute or two just blinking at the screen like an idiot. Me? Intriguing?

«*Are you there?*»

Flustered now, I typed.

Yes. No one ever called me "intriguing" before. I'm really not all that interesting. Just a clerk who likes to go to museums and art galleries when I get to the city. And sew quilts and read novels in my spare time.

«*Please believe me when I tell you that makes you most interesting to me. The women I know have no work, no skills, and no interest in art.*»

At that, my brows shot up. I could not let that pass unchallenged.

That is difficult to imagine. Surely the women you know are all cultured and educated?

«*Their primary focus is fashion and pursuit of a rich husband. Being still unmarried, I often find myself a hare running from hounds.*»

I snickered at the image of the handsome prince in snowy robes fleeing across a desert with a bevy of coifed beauties hot on his heels like hunting dogs.

Well, I typed, *I'm not after a husband, rich or poor, and my idea of fashion is the most comfortable shoes I can find to fit my size-eight feet.*

«*You are very funny. May I invite you to chat*

with me by telephone?»

I balked. Exchanging a few private messages seemed safe: faceless and voiceless and as personal as a machine recording. A phone call, on the other hand, would make him real. And make my tendency to stammer over the airwaves all too clear.

«Perhaps I am too forward.»

I actually trembled as my fingers tapped the keyboard. *I really can't afford to make phone calls.* Even before I finished, I recognized how lame that sounded when he would be calling me and taking the charges. For a moment, I closed my eyes on a groan. Then, I decided to admit the truth and, when I opened my eyes to type, I caught his response.

«I promise that I will accept all costs for the opportunity to hear your voice. I imagine it is musical.»

Musical. I huffed without humour. About as musical as an alley cat in heat. With another resigned sigh, I replied.

Okay. I confess. I am the world's worst phone pal. I get all tongue-tied on the telephone. Always have. No idea why. I added, *And I just don't feel comfortable getting so familiar so fast.*

«I understand.»

I was about to go back to checking my home page when I saw another entry.

«Would you prefer e-mail, until we know each other better?»

My teeth worried my upper lip a few seconds while I thought about it. Finally I typed, *Sure. I guess that would be okay.*

At once, he entered an address and a request that I contact him. I copied the address to a document file and promised to send off an e-letter that day. It was only after I had closed out of social and done a web search of Prince Ali that I recalled that there had been more than one account with his handle. Was there another royal by that name? Or had some impostor made a page?

I reopened social. After scanning the prince's "official" page, I checked the others bearing similar names, one at a time. Some belonged to men with significantly different profile photos. A few were surely relatives, so closely did they resemble the prince, but they were older or younger and their posts proclaimed widely differing professions and interests.

Two, though, appeared to be offshoots of the official page, with images of the prince—or at least of someone who could be the man's twin. These bore only a handful of posts that qualified as political, the majority of them displaying his love of horses and airplanes and dancing with beautiful women. I cringed at the latter. I could never compete with gorgeous celebrities. At that thought I wondered why on earth I would even for an instant entertain the notion of a relationship with someone of his status, and thousands of miles away to boot.

"You're losin' it," I muttered to myself.

It was with visions of the handsome black-haired Arab gliding across a ballroom floor with a stunning blonde that I opened my favourite e-mail account and composed my first letter.

FROM: PRINCE ALI BIN RASHID BIN AMIN AL ASH-SHEIKH
To: Connie Tyson
Subject: Questions
Ms. Tyson,

I see that you are a prudent woman. The many problems of Western society lead one to wariness; this I understand.

As to your questions, I maintain an official page for my position as heir apparent and government functionary. You may imagine that it is screened by men of my father's choosing who ensure that my public image reflects well upon my family. This page shows my people what my father and I do for them and the future we work toward.

I keep a second, private page for fun. Through it I have made friends around the world, friends with whom I can "let my hair down," as you say.

There is a third page, I know, that purports to be my own, and I thank you for bringing it to my attention. I am negotiating to have it removed and my father has ordered an investigation of the impostor. I hope to resolve the matter soon.

But it is not yet corrected, and that is why I have asked you to contact me through other means. I regret the imposition, but it is necessary to ensure privacy. It is possible that the man impersonating me is able to hijack my communications, I am told. Having only moderate technical expertise, I prefer to err on the side of caution, as you do.

Therefore, let me express my joy that you have chosen to converse with me even by such sterile channels. I would be most honoured to call you my friend and I assure you that I am yours.

  I regret that I must cut this message short. My father requires my presence.
Peace be unto you.
Ali

I STARED AT THE MESSAGE a long time, reading and rereading it. Finally, I decided to accept this man at face value. We would probably never call each other, much less meet in person. What harm could there be in exchanging occasional letters?

CHAPTER 2

Hook, line...

"HELLO. I'M YOUR NEIGHBOUR, in three-twelve."

The tallish man with wavy brown hair, grey eyes, smiling face, and slim build offered his hand, but then realized my fumbling effort to take it pointed to poor judgement on his part. At once, he grabbed the upper box I almost dropped as he added, "Graham. Graham Urquhart."

"Connie Tyson," I replied and slipped my key into the doorknob to open my new apartment. After a run-in with a very drunk

Jean-Guy, I had decided to move somewhere, anywhere, away from the town I had grown up in. I had transferred easily enough because the boss back home liked me, but he liked the new girl with the big boobs better and an opening had come up in the city. So, Tom put in a good word.

My new neighbour and I lumbered through the doorway into the empty space reeking of fresh paint, found the kitchen, and deposited our burdens on the green Formica counter that smelled of industrial cleanser. Hands now free, I extended one and we shook.

"Nice to meet you," he said. "Need more help?"

I hesitated. "Um, well...."

He held up both hands, palms toward me, and responded, "If you'd rather not trust a complete stranger, I can't blame you. Especially when you're new in town."

"How did you know that?" I demanded, instantly suspicious.

"Uh...." He pointed to my tee.

Glancing down, I groaned inwardly at my stupidity. Nothing like an old highschool-team booster shirt to tell the world where you're from. Rolling my eyes and then meeting his as heat, and no doubt redness, rose from my midsection to the top of my head, I said, "Thanks for not saying, 'Duh!'"

He grinned. "I'm from Barry's Bay, myself." He tilted his head. "So, what brings you to The Big City?" He emphasized the last words with finger quotations.

Without thought, I answered, "Too many men I'm either related to or divorced from." (I always was too honest for my own good. And my mouth tended to work faster than my brain, besides.) I noticed the sudden coolness in his eyes and stiffening of his posture. Trying to salvage what might at least become a casual friendship in a city where I knew no one else, I rushed to ask with an injection of cheer, "How about you?"

"No exes," he replied. "But too many relatives and not enough job opportunities."

I gestured toward the door. A carload of garment bags and luggage still needed fetching. On the way out, I inquired, "So, what do you do, if you don't mind my asking?"

"Government service," he declared with a return of his boyish grin.

"Ah, taxman," I quipped. "Guess I'd better mind my P's and Q's. And my T4's and T5's."

He chuckled as we pushed out the back door to the parking lot. Then, he eyed my rust-spotted beige four-door sitting in a puddle of snowmelt as I unlocked it and pulled out the pair of suitcases I'd picked up at a thrift store.

"This baby's been around a few years," he remarked as he plucked up the luggage unbidden.

I got no bad vibes from him, so I decided not to object to his assistance.

"Yeah," I admitted as I piled dress bags over my left arm. "It was my dad's once upon a time. Then my brother's. But I'm afraid I'm not nearly as good at maintenance as they were."

"Well, the great thing about the city is public transit. When your car heaves its last gasp, just get yourself a bus pass."

"I will," I said. "But I hope that'll be a few years off, yet." I slammed the door shut with my hip as I wrestled with the heap of slippery plastic bags and headed for the building's side entrance.

"Let me get the door," Graham volunteered. "Then, we'll take the elevator."

I blew shaggy chestnut-brown bangs out of my eyes. "Thanks. I really can use the help."

THE FIRST MONTH went well enough. I got used to the peculiarities of my stove; the erratic hours of the neighbour across the hall; the new phone number and address that needed to be given to all my friends and relatives back home as well as to my bank, utility companies, and employer. I settled in at work and got acquainted with colleagues, procedures, customers, and office politics. So far, I had made no enemies and only a few mistakes. And I bought a bus pass to conserve gas.

Graham Urquhart had taken to offering help with my car maintenance and suggesting casual outings together to explore the city. I had to admit he was a nice guy: kind, attentive, attractive. But I had had my fill of men. Or at least of relationships. Too complicated. Too much chance of heartbreak. So I kept it friendly and cool. No kiss at the door. No expensive dinners. No bars or parties. No sex.

But I had Ali waiting in cyberspace—if I could re-establish contact. Between the craziness of organizing my move and packing and installing myself in a new apartment, and the sudden inexplicable crashing of my laptop that required a trip to a repair shop, once I found one, and a subsequent interminable wait while the techs figured out what was wrong and what to do about it, I had been unable to access any of my online accounts. Phone calls and second-hand social messages had assured family and friends that I had not departed this earth, but connecting to the prince was limited to two options, neither of them currently available. Though I told myself repeatedly that it didn't matter if he gave up on me, I couldn't fool myself into believing I would not be disappointed if he did.

GRAHAM WAS OUT OF TOWN, according to a note on a slip of paper shoved under my door. A twinge of disappointment surprised me, because I had been telling myself he was just a friend, a buddy to go to museums and outdoor concerts with. But I crumpled the note and tossed it into the recycling box in the kitchen on my way to deposit my purse on my dresser and change into shorts before I started supper.

About an hour later, after I had reheated a portion of the spicy three-cheese lasagne I'd made and frozen the week before, and after a quiet meal with a glass of the red wine I kept only because I was too stubborn to toss the putrid stuff when I'd paid almost twenty dollars for it, and after a thorough wash of the dishes and tidying of the kitchen, I got a call. When Don from Don's Computer Sales and Service informed me I could pick up my machine anytime, I grabbed my purse and raced out to drive the thirty or so blocks and pull to the kerb in front of the repair shop just before Friday late closing. My heart skipped at the figure on the invoice, but I handed over my credit card and hoped I could pay off the debt within two months, three max.

My whole body seemed to sing as I drove home against the traffic headed for downtown restaurants and theatres. Twenty minutes later, once all peripherals had been set up and tested, I sat at my laptop and accessed the internet. First, as always, I checked personal e-mails and deleted the solicitations for money from charities of dubious credibility and political parties of even less trustworthiness. (I kept promising myself I'd unsubscribe to them all, but I somehow never made that small effort. As usual, I cursed as I consigned the lot to cyber oblivion.)

But there was nothing from my prince.

With a dismayed sigh, I skimmed through a few news feeds and shook my head at the latest ridiculous ballyhoo out of Hollywood. Finally, I logged into my social account and scanned posts from friends and relatives and from the pages I'd taken a shine to. My heart galloped when I spotted several notifications that Ali had sent a message.

The most recent read: «*I have not heard from you for weeks. Are you well?*»

Sorry, I replied to the message that was eight days old, *I have moved to the city, my laptop decided to stop working, and I've been unable to use the internet at work—it's very busy at this time of year, and my boss has been keeping an eye on me while I settle in. But I did send an e-mail just before moving day and I received no reply.*

To my surprise, he answered immediately.

«*Yes. My account had been compromised and our security people instantly confiscated my computers and telephones to ensure there are no diseases present.*»

I snickered. For someone so obviously well educated, he sometimes surprised me with wrong words or mangled phrases.

Viruses. Computer viruses, I corrected.

«*Viruses, yes. I have been in Europe and using more French than English, of late.*»

Sounds exciting.

«*No. Boring. Politics and tours of factories, for the most part. I am glad to be home and able to speak with you again. I have missed you.*»

I actually flushed with pleasure. After a moment's indecision, I responded in kind. *I missed you, too. I'm glad you didn't give up and forget about me.*

«*I could never forget you. And this separation has shown me how important you have become in my life.*»

Before I could think of a reply to the unexpected declaration, another message came through.

«*I must go now. I will e-mail you this evening, my dear.*»

For several minutes, I stared at the screen. My dear. Despite my better judgement, I found myself imagining that I might meet the handsome Prince Ali bin Rashid bin Amin Al ash-Sheikh. And maybe even....

THE TIME DIFFERENCE often made quick communication impossible, especially by e-mail. And his work and mine added to the lag. But my early-morning check the next day revealed a new letter. I ignored the other mail and the aroma of perking coffee to open his missive and read with a thrill.

🖥

FROM: PRINCE ALI BIN RASHID BIN AMIN AL ASH-SHEIKH
To: Connie Tyson
Subject: Joyful greetings
My dear Connie,

How I have missed you! I am so happy to know you are well and you have not forgotten me, as I had feared. Please believe me when I tell you that my heart soars to know you care for me as I care for you.

I would ask to telephone you, but my minders are closely monitoring my cell and I prefer they not hear of my feelings for you at this time. There are too many eager ears in the palace and my father and I have enemies.

I hasten to add that you need not worry for my safety. My guards are absolutely loyal; of that I am certain. Nonetheless, the ever-thorough General al-Tammar has tightened security against possible threats, especially now that I am to visit your country and the United States of America in a month's time.

It is my fervent wish that I may meet you

when we arrive. Already I have asked my secretary to ensure several free hours for that purpose. He does not know why I wish it, and I will tell no one until the last moment, lest the General forbid our tryst. I could not bear to be thwarted.

In the meantime, if you allow it, I will ask your aid in this endeavour and another. My journey across the ocean has at its heart a goal of historic significance and of great benefit to all the peoples of the world. You might well assume this statement to be mere bombastic hyperbole, the florid rhetoric of a politician or the foolish attempts of a love-struck man to impress the woman he desires. But I assure you that my words contain profound truth.

Please promise me that you will consider meeting with me.
Peace be unto you.
Your Ali

🖥

AGAIN I STARED at the screen before me, my mind and heart racing. He was actually coming and he wanted to meet me! My hands shook as I logged out, forgot breakfast (but at least remembered to turn off the coffee machine and lock my door), and headed for work in a daze.

CHAPTER 3

Sinker

MY NEW BOSS, BILL, finally decided I needed no extra supervision. For that, I was ecstatic not just because I had found his hovering and constant inspecting of my work insulting, but because I wanted to check my personal e-mails for updates from Ali. Not that I expected any for a few days, maybe a week or more. But Ali's mention that he might require some help from me had finally sunk in by the time I arrived at the office.

As I began my day's tasks, I mulled his assertion. What could he need from me?

Maps, he could get online and probably through his generals, as well. Plane and train schedules were also freely available, and he would likely be using a private jet, anyway. Try as I might, I could not think of a single thing I could do for him that could not be done better by someone on his own staff.

Finally, I decided he simply wanted me to arrange, from my end, a place for us to meet. I could do that easily and no one would ever suspect who I was really making the reservation for. No peeping palace spies and no international enemies would have a clue what he was up to.

Yes, that must be it.

A SHIVER THAT COMBINED excitement and alarm shot up my spine when I received his next message at 6 a.m. the following day. The e-mail read: "I must ask that you contact me at noon, your time, for I have a special request. I must know your answer and my schedule allows only a small window in which we may directly connect."

I agreed because I expected to be at my

desk until half past before taking the late lunch shift.

At noon I smiled to Bill and the big boss Greg Donnegan, who was visiting from company headquarters, as the pair in slacks and sport coats left through the glass front door flanked by wide windows, both men oblivious as they talked politics and headed for lunch at a local café. My pasted smile no doubt resembled a grimace by the time the chatty Natalie and Linda sauntered away from their desks, round the end of the counter that ran the length of the room, and out the side door that led to the washrooms and kitchenette and staff lounge as the digital clock on my screen registered 12:04.

Alone at last! But wouldn't you know it: A customer called just then to ask for an extra order of boxes and packing tape for his shipment.

I was shaking with anxiety and anger as I finally opened my personal e-mail account and scrolled impatiently to find the letter from Ali.

FROM: CONNIE TYSON
Reply to: Prince Ali bin Rashid bin Amin Al ash-Sheikh
Subject: Request

Dear Ali:

I am so sorry it took this long to get back to you. It has been a zoo here.
Your friend,
Connie

From: Prince Ali bin Rashid bin Amin Al ash-Sheikh
Reply to: Connie Tyson
Subject: Request
My dear Connie:

I am so glad to hear from you. I, too, have been living in a zoo, today.

For that reason, I have little time and I will simply ask a favour of you. One of my men will come to your place of business tomorrow in order to hire a vehicle. Please expedite the necessary paperwork.

He will announce himself as John Crozier and pay by credit card for a large truck to ship medicines from a factory in your country to a distributor in Baltimore, Maryland. Please believe me when I tell you these are truly remarkable drugs, discovered by a scientist in my father's employ. One of the key ingredients is

made in my own country from a local herb.
    Will you help me?
Your faithful servant,
Ali

From: Connie Tyson
Reply to: Prince Ali bin Rashid bin Amin Al ash-Sheikh
Subject: Request
Dear Ali:
    Of course I will help. John Crozier. When should I expect him?
Connie

From: Prince Ali bin Rashid bin Amin Al ash-Sheikh
Reply to: Connie Tyson
Subject: Request
My dear Connie:
    I am told he will arrive later today and present himself when your company opens in the morning. He will call ahead this evening to begin the arrangements. I know that your work day

ends at 6 p.m. Can you linger to take his call?
Ali

From: Connie Tyson
Reply to: Prince Ali bin Rashid bin Amin Al ash-Sheikh
Subject: Request
Dear Ali:
    Yes. I will be waiting.
Connie

From: Prince Ali bin Rashid bin Amin Al ash-Sheikh
Reply to: Connie Tyson
Subject: Request
Sweet Connie:
    I and many others are eternally in your debt for this assistance.
    Further, I wait with bated breath for our meeting. Painful will be the slow passage of the coming month.
Peace be unto you.
Your devoted Ali

I CLOSED OUT QUICKLY as one of the drivers strode in and deposited a batch of forms. The afternoon crawled, thereafter, as I went through the motions of taking my lunch break, inputting data, tending clients, filing papers, and answering phones while Natalie and Linda discussed Natalie's upcoming hot date, painted their nails in a rainbow of colours, groused when asked to handle the phones while I ran to the washroom, and flirted with the new driver, Marty (an arrogant little prick who figured women should fall into his bed if he snapped his fingers).

At closing time, I tarried at the file cabinet, sorting misfiled folders and pretending to look for one in particular. No one paid much attention to me, all happy just to head for home or for a bar. At a quarter after six, Bill wanted to lock up. Knowing he would tell me to leave whatever work remained till morning, I dashed to the Ladies to give me an excuse to stay a little longer.

"Go out the back way," he called as he walked by the lavatory after securing the front entrance.

"Okay," I called back.

When I heard the rear door clack shut, I

peeked outside. Then, I hurried to the office and sat with pulse racing as I waited for John Crozier's call. I nearly jumped out of my skin when the strident ring broke the unaccustomed silence five minutes later. Immediately, I grabbed the receiver.

"Donnegan's Cartage," I answered breathlessly.

A deep, sexy voice without a trace of accent replied, "I need a truck for a week today."

"No problem, sir. May I ask your name?"

"John Crozier." He spelled it for me.

Then, he asked, "What's your name, honey?"

The endearment would have irritated me did I not believe the query was meant to ensure he was talking to the right woman. I answered simply, "Connie Tyson."

"We have a mutual friend."

"Yes."

Then, he gave me the details of his order and I filled out the myriad company and Customs forms he would need and e-mailed a note to Bill so he would assign a van first thing in the morning. Finally, I exited the rear door, crossed the huge parking lot where massive transport trucks awaited their next run, nodded to the night guards who patrolled the premises, and strolled to the bus stop feeling light as air.

CHAPTER 4

Reeled in

I WAS HALFWAY HOME by the time I remembered that I had left my empty lunchbox in the kitchenette and might have forgotten to turn off the coffee machine, besides. Rolling my eyes at my lapse, I considered just continuing to my apartment and hoping one of the night guards would turn off the machine. I could always go out for lunch tomorrow.

But I reached up and yanked the cord to ring the bell that would signal the bus driver to let me off at the next stop. I just couldn't take the chance Hal and Gino would fail to notice the little red light in the kitchen. The pot might boil dry and melt the damned plastic lid, or the cord might short and start a fire, or who-knew-what-else could happen if I didn't go back and check. (I usually checked stoves, locks, and my wallet with an equal sense of impending doom.)

At the next intersection, I hopped off the northbound Number Three, crossed the street, and stood waiting for the southbound Three. With a heavy sigh, I noted ahead the receding shape of the bus I'd missed five minutes before and I stepped out of the cool late-spring wind into the plexiglass shelter that smelled of stale urine to wait for the next one. I spent a half-hour cursing myself both for my forgetfulness and for my obsessive need to check what probably needed no checking.

THE STREETLIGHTS BLINKED ON just as I stepped off the bus. I walked from one pool of pink glow to the next and around the corner toward the low front building of Donnegan's Cartage. The light in the office did not surprise me: I figured Hal kept a few of the fluorescents running to discourage vandalism and pilferage, just as the company always maintained plenty of illumination around the parking lot and the massive garage lest somebody decide to abscond with a truck or a few litres of gas. After all, a heavy transport van, even an older model, was a tempting target for auto thieves, as were the racks of spare parts in the outbuildings. And with gas prices skyrocketing, even an average car-owner might be tempted to "borrow" a tankful when no one was looking.

Standing at the front door, I scanned past the counter that bisected the outer office to find no sign of movement. From there, all I could see of the side corridor that led to the kitchen was the plastered corner, and I felt relieved that no flickering orange glow from beyond it signalled a blazing disaster in the making.

I tugged at the door, forgetting it was locked, and then shook my head at yet another lapse. Fortunately, I had memorized the code to open the service entrance, so I strode quickly along to the side, in a hurry to get out of the increasingly strong and chilly wind. Under the glare of an overhead light, I started to punch the numbers into the keypad, but I stopped on hearing voices.

Frowning and blinking, aware that none of the speakers sounded like Hal or his partner Gino, I stepped to the rear corner of the admin building, hugging the masonry, and I peered toward the noises that did not belong. What I saw widened my eyes and wrenched a gasp from my lips: Two guards lay sprawled on the ground next to the open garage door; the newest of the trucks sat parked at the entrance; one man lay on a wheeled board under the chassis, his feet visible between two sets of tires; and Marty O'Connor turned from where he was tinkering under the hood to fix me with a hard stare.

My heart skipped and I whirled to run for it, only to smack into a wall of flesh. Looking up with wild eyes and racing pulse, I beheld the most beautiful man I had ever seen: He had to be six-three or –four; his body, judging by the impact of mine with his, bore a rock-hard musculature many men would kill for; darkly tanned skin emphasized the smooth planes of his face; and even shadowed beneath his brows, his eyes shone startlingly blue. On some purely primal level I noticed that heat and a scent of musky aftershave emanated from him.

"Going somewhere?" a deep voice purred casually as large hands seized my upper arms.

I should have screamed while I had the chance. Instead, I whispered, "Who are you? What did you do to Hal and Gino?"

One brow rose and his mouth curled wryly as he pushed me backward into the light that bathed the parking lot. "They're not dead," he assured me. "Just...sleeping."

I swallowed hard in a throat suddenly dry. I had heard that voice not so long ago, on the phone. "What-what-what...?"

"What are we doing?" John Crozier finished for me. His smile broadened, his eyes glinting with amusement. "We're loading up for our journey to Washington, of course."

At that, I frowned and blinked. Washington? His shipment was supposed to go to Baltimore. Next week.

"Why did you come back?" he asked with a tilt of his head.

Still blinking in bewilderment, I answered lamely, "I forgot to turn off the coffee machine."

A low chuckle rumbled up from his belly to swell to a thunderous guffaw that shook his shoulders and crinkled his eyes. His laughter had not quite died before he abruptly lifted me off the ground with an arm around my waist and planted a rough kiss, its insistence made the more demanding when his free hand pressed my head to keep me pinned.

He started walking.

Owl-eyed with astonishment, I simply hung there a moment, my feet dangling a foot or so off the ground as he carried me. Then I heard the giggles from metres away and realized someone was walking by along the sidewalk. Instantly, I began to struggle. But the passersby might not see Hal and Gino from their vantage point, and John Crozier (or whatever his name really was) obviously intended onlookers to believe he and I were lovers saying goodbye before he drove off in the truck.

He had turned away from the street, his Herculean bulk blocking view of my desperate efforts to free myself. All too soon, the snickers and chatter faded. But the man kept his mouth clamped to mine, muffling my panicked screams as he hauled me around the end of the vehicle and through its open rear door, keeping me immobilized until he reached the farthest wall of the rig's long box and summarily shoved me against it. The impact knocked the wind out of me.

In the gloomy interior, his hands circled my throat. I stared in horror at the face I could not see as I waited for his fingers to squeeze tighter. He leaned forward, hovering so close I could feel the warmth of his breath on my lips and the heat of his body through his dark cotton tee and denim jeans.

"A pity," he said. "I had been looking forward to a more romantic meeting, sweet Connie. But your untimely arrival tonight has forced a change of plans."

His grip loosened and his palms slid down over my shoulders, across my chest to find my breasts, and then farther to my hips and around to my backside all the while he continued, "Nevertheless, we may have a little time to spend together before...."

Suddenly, one of his hands clasped my throat again and powerful fingers pinched painfully. As I blacked out, I heard him finish with nonchalance bordering on disinterest, "But not tonight."

CHAPTER 5

Landed

I WAS NO LONGER IN THE TRUCK, I realized. And I was not bound. Still reeling from the pain of my earlier attempt to rise, I rolled to one side and gingerly tried again from another position. I managed to prop myself on one elbow. Then, once my head stopped spinning and my stomach settled, I slowly pushed up to sit and peer into the blackness.

Gradually, I began to perceive shapes. Boxes; I was surrounded by boxes. And sounds;

there were distant rumbles, though I could not discern what produced them.

Water. All at once I recognized the stench that assailed my nostrils: stagnant water. And oil. And diesel. And urine. Was the last mine? My pants clung with cold wetness, and I hoped I had not peed myself.

But embarrassment over incontinence was surely of no importance given that I would likely not live much longer. And perhaps such a physical mishap would make me less desirable to libidinous captors. Not that being used by them before they killed me would amount to much, either, I supposed. But that did seem to be what John Crozier had had in mind.

Then, I remembered: "Sweet Connie," he had murmured.

A jolt shot through me.

Were Crozier and Ali one and the same? Had I been played so completely?

My mind raced through every message, every e-mail. As I finished scanning my mental filing system, my head nodded of its own accord. If the two were not one, they had certainly shared the cyber communications. I felt sick at an image of one or more men laughing at the silly woman so desperate for love that she had lapped up every endearment and acquiesced to every request. It occurred to me I had been extraordinarily gullible in accepting statements and explanations that must seem preposterous to anyone else. To anyone with a lick of sense.

I closed my eyes on tears of shame.

But my sobs subsided when I began to wonder exactly what Ali/Crozier intended. Washington. Another jolt raced up my spine at a suspicion: Did he/they plan to set off a bomb or something?

Marty. I recalled that Marty was one of them. Between getting him into Donnegan's and softening me up with e-mails, their scheme must have been in the works for months. But how was it they had targeted me? Or did I turn out to be just the most useful choice among a slew of women they had contacted? Donnegan's, too, may have been one of many companies they had scouted. So they probably narrowed the field until they found the perfect pawns for their game.

At a sudden vision of Hal and Gino lying on the tarmac, my stomach flipped. I quelled nausea, but let tears flow freely as I wondered if the two guards were still alive. They were not friends, indeed they barely qualified as acquaintances, but I could not bear to think my stupidity had cost them their lives.

As I shifted on the concrete to alleviate the ache in my rear, my mind drifted back to the question of where I might be at this moment. Had we crossed into America yet?

I knew from jokes and anecdotes I had overheard from the drivers that there were "back ways" into and out of the US, roads used only by smugglers wishing to avoid the Customs and Security checkpoints along the border. No doubt Marty or Crozier had surveyed them all. So, if we were not on American soil yet, we soon would be.

A screech drew my gaze as a door opened to admit blinding light. I squinted and blinked.

"Ah, you're awake," said Crozier. "Good. We will be leaving in a few minutes."

"In broad daylight?" I gasped.

He chuckled. "Yes, little Connie. In broad daylight. No one will see us." His tone hardened. "And no one will hear you; so, do not bother to call for help."

He tilted his head as he approached. "Then again, it matters not whether you scream. No one will hear." I saw the flash of teeth as he bent to grab my arm and haul me to a stand. His arms wrapped me and his breath caressed my cheek as he added softly, "At least, no one who will care."

CHAPTER 6

Struggling on the line

HE HAD BOUND MY HANDS AND FEET this time and I tried in vain to ease the pressure on my wrists and ankles; the ropes were rubbing me raw. Wouldn't you know a trio of terrorists—or whatever they were—would be eco-conscious enough to use real hemp rope instead of the artificial substitute so easily obtained in hardware stores and so much gentler on the skin.

But at least I wasn't rolling around on the floor and getting bumped and battered about. It was by no means comfortable sitting with my back to a cold, hard wall and my arse digging into the ribbed pattern of the metal floor, mind. But beggars could not be choosers, as Mom always said.

When I shifted again, I felt something firm but flexible. Twisting to grope by my hip, I found my purse. At first it made no sense to me that they hadn't left my handbag behind. Then, I realized if anyone found it my disappearance might be connected with the theft of the truck and maybe even give away the route my kidnappers were taking. That police might assume I had stolen the vehicle crossed my mind, but I dismissed the notion as unlikely given my lack of appropriate driver training. My having been abducted or murdered by the thieves was the logical conclusion.

With crossed hands, I probed my environment in the darkness, quickly detecting wooden pallets to either side. I fervently hoped they would not slide to crush me. Each was piled with bundles that stretched up beyond my reach, the rounded objects all wrapped in plastic sheeting and strapped down with wide, stiff plastic ties. The goods gave a little when I pressed. These, I was sure, were window dressing: something to show cops or transport inspectors should the rig be pulled over. No one would find drugs or bombs or any other contraband.

On the other hand, I had to admit, a bound woman would not be overlooked by any authorities. Or even bystanders. With a pang of unease, I wondered if my captors would kill anyone curious enough to peek inside the van. And I snorted a mirthless chuckle at the brief hope that no one would put them to the test, that all would go smoothly for Crozier et al—in which case I had little hope of surviving this journey.

Damned if they do, damned if they don't.

MY EYES FLUTTERED OPEN and my flushed face pulled plastic with it as I jerked away from the roll of soft stuff against which I had fallen. It dawned on me as I straightened that I must have nodded off. But the drone of tires on pavement had ceased, as had the swaying motion that had kept me on edge mile after mile as my body tried to compensate for the assault on its equilibrium. Simply staying upright had been exhausting; no wonder I drifted to sleep.

I needed to pee. And I needed a drink. Food would have been nice, too, though I was not sure I could stomach much.

"I need to go to the bathroom!" I shouted as forcefully as my dry mouth and general fatigue would allow.

After a minute or so I tried again. "I really need to go to the bathroom, asshole!"

Though I thought I might no longer need one if I dared to shout again, I opened my mouth to scream. Just then, the door at the far end of the truck swung open to admit daylight and a looming figure. The look on Crozier's face shut me up instantly, and my heart sped as he stalked to me along the narrow aisle between the pallets secured to left and right. Maybe he didn't like to be called "asshole." I cringed, expecting a slap that would leave my cheek bruised for days.

When he reached me, he dropped to one knee and pulled a knife that snapped open as it cleared his pocket. My eyes flew wide as horrific scenarios involving blood and pain flashed through my mind. But instead of cutting me, he slipped the blade between my ankles to slit the ropes with astounding ease.

"Listen carefully, little Connie," he hissed. "There are people outside, people whose lives depend upon your cooperation."

As the bonds at my wrists fell away, he locked my gaze and assured, "We will kill them all, including the children, if you give the remotest hint that anything is amiss. Do you understand?"

My breath stilled as he pierced me with those icy blue orbs.

"Do you understand?" he repeated, his tone quiet but intense.

I nodded slightly and swallowed with difficulty.

That settled, he inspected the welts on my skin and grunted.

"I really need to go to the bathroom," I whispered.

He glanced up a moment, then he said brusquely, "First I'll bandage those." With that, he rose and strode out.

I was biting my lips and squeezing my lower half as tightly as I could when he returned an interminable minute or two later. With a practised hand, he wound gauze that smelled of antiseptic around my wrists and tied it off. Finally, he pulled me to a stand and led me out to the public washroom at the side of the gas station that sat beside a lonely two-lane road flanked by dense forest.

I EMERGED from the small but clean lavatory still aching from the strain to my bladder and sphincter but happy that the water I had been sitting in earlier had been just that: water. My clothes were rumpled and less than pristine, but I did not stink of urine.

Around front of the old house that now doubled as a rest stop and tuck shop for travellers, three squealing preschoolers raced about with several dogs yapping at their heels as an elderly man leaned on an old Coca Cola fridge on the porch, eyeing us and chewing a stalk of grass while a younger one I guessed to be his son filled the truck's huge tank with diesel. An odour of onions frying in butter competed with the reek of fuel that overwhelmed the clean scent of pine from the surrounding woods.

"Good thing we'll be gettin' another tankful tomorrah," commented a plump matron with wisps of grey hair floating around her freckled face. "Don't get many big rigs out here. Most take the Interstate."

Crozier smiled winningly and reached an arm around my shoulder to pull me close. "We thought we'd take the scenic route." He looked down to me and added, "Right honey?"

I forced a smile and nodded. "Right."

The woman's sharp eyes noted my hesitance, and Crozier noted her reaction. At once, he said, "This is my wife's first trip and she's not used to it yet." He squeezed my shoulder as he added, "Already better than that first day, though, eh sweetheart?"

"Right. Yes," I responded with as much cheer as I could muster. "Much better."

"I can give ya somethin' for the motion sickness," the lady offered.

At a painful pinch, I rushed to say, "No. No, thank you. I'll be fine. Already getting used to it."

"Well, if you're sure."

At my emphatic head bob and wide smile, she smiled back with a tolerant expression that conveyed her certainty that I would be green in the face all the way to wherever I was headed.

The only good thing about that encounter was the kidnappers' need to put me up front, in the cab with them, in order to convince the locals that I was a participant, not a prisoner.

CROZIER HAD PUSHED ME into the rear seat and climbed in after. I don't doubt it was significantly less comfortable for him in the cramped space that forced him to sit at an angle to accommodate his long legs, but it couldn't have been nearly as bad as sitting on the hard floor among the pallets had been for me.

When Marty pulled us onto the road again, the behemoth beside me glanced over casually and said, "You did well. It would have been a shame to have to kill a whole family."

"But murdering a city full of families is okay by you?" Seething at the choice he had forced me to make and at the goal I suspected he and his cohorts worked toward, I threw him a cold glare. "That's what this is about, isn't it? To blow up Washington in the name of...what? God?"

It may have been foolish bravado I would soon rue, but at that moment I was too angry to hold my tongue.

The man called Joaquin turned, bared his teeth, and raised a hand, but Crozier held up his own hand. "Watch the road," he commanded. "We cannot afford to lose our way."

When the fierce-eyed Latino shifted to resume his position as navigator, muttering what

I guessed to be derogatory comments in Spanish, Crozier leaned back into the crook between the edge of the seat and the door and eyed me a moment. Presently, he said, "I assure you we will not blow up a city."

"Fine," I replied sardonically. "You're going to all this trouble, risking a lifetime in jail or maybe a shootout with cops, just to deliver a supply of blankets."

Feeling my oats, I added, "And the cops WILL be looking for you down here. The paperwork in the computer—"

He cut me off. "What paperwork?"

His cool, confident smile chilled me.

"There is no paperwork in your files or on your computer, my dear Connie."

My face no doubt revealed my realization. He nodded as he clarified, "Everything has been erased." He added, "And the disappearance of the truck will be considered an ordinary theft by a ring already well known to police."

My heart sank. Voice as tremulous as I felt, I protested, "Even so, they'll be looking for me when I don't show up for work."

Again, he shocked me with an oh-so-casual comment. "You e-mailed your boss that you are ill, my dear Connie."

Before I could respond with another desperately hopeful statement, he added, "And you have left a message on your social accounts that you are feeling unwell and plan to stay in bed for..." he waved a hand, "several days."

With a triumphant smile I wanted to scratch from his face, he concluded, "No one will be looking for you for quite some time, my dear. And by the time they do, you will be—"

This time it was I who cut him off. "Dead."

He made a show of looking me over and then he reached to caress my cheek with a curled forefinger.

"Not necessarily," he said. He seemed to be mulling it over a few seconds before he went on, "Although there is a much larger market for younger stock, there are still a few men of...stature," he grinned at the word, "who prefer mutton to lamb."

My breath stilled as I stared at him. Suddenly aware of every nerve in my body, I wondered whether I would rather be murdered outright or enslaved to some old fart who would probably tire of me in a few months, or maybe weeks, and kill me anyway. I had never been any great shakes in bed, at least not according to those I'd slept with; so, I didn't think my value in the sex market would be very high.

His tone dripping honey as his hand drifted boldly from my face to my neck and on to tease my breast, Crozier murmured, "Of course, I may have use for you, myself, sweet Connie."

Gaze meeting mine, he said, "Either way, my dear, you will never again have need to feel lonely."

His smile widened to a wolfish grin under eyes that bored directly to my soul.

CHAPTER 7

Off the hook

MARTY AND JOAQUIN TOOK TURNS at the wheel through day and night. We stopped occasionally to water the roadside grass, the men utterly unabashed to whip out their members in front of me. I was afforded no privacy and endured their speculative stares as I pulled off my pants and relieved myself. But they apparently had no time to indulge in a sampling of their purloined goods, because none of them touched me. Even Crozier, sitting with me in the back seat, refrained from any further lewd suggestions or behaviours. After a time, my fearful wariness waned and I fell asleep with head pillowed on a black canvas duffel stuffed into the corner by the door.

Eventually, I woke to the smell of manure and found we were now passing through farm country. Still on back roads, we slowed behind tractors and through villages on our way to a haze on the horizon. Now and then, we stopped for gas and food and bathroom breaks, always with a reminder to me that the lives of innocent people depended upon my discretion and obedience.

I estimated that had we taken any of the normal truck routes, we'd have been in DC days ago. Nonetheless, we soon passed from rural to suburban landscape and saw nothing but asphalt, traffic, and buildings of various sizes from then on.

The sun kissed the treetops in the west as we turned again somewhere shy of the sprawling city, or maybe in a section of it, onto a winding road that continued past impressive estates surrounded by vast lawns and edged by trees and ornate fences. Eventually, we pulled into a lane and, to my surprise, the gate opened to admit the van. I supposed anyone seeing our arrival might assume this was a moving vehicle or delivery truck and take no particular notice, though the hour was late.

Joaquin drove around back to the servants' and tradesmen's entrance that opened onto a cobbled court stretching from the three-storey grey stone house to several outbuildings, some broad, some small, all low and roofed with silvered cedar shingles.

My guess that nobody was home, not even employees, soon proved correct. Crozier grabbed my arm and manhandled me into the mansion, through the kitchen, up two flights of stairs, and along a hall carpeted by oriental runners to a dusky bedroom where the furniture had been covered with white sheets and the curtains beneath the canopy of the huge four-poster bed kept dust off the mattress. He pushed me into a wing chair by the Rumford fireplace on the side wall, and then strode to reach behind heavy draperies to the latticed windows beyond and tested each of the sets of casements that flanked the bed. All were locked.

I fished, "Is this Prince Ali's American home? Did he send you?"

Crozier regarded me with a wry smile and

assessing eyes. "Still not understanding, I see."

He stepped to me and bent, clasping and leaning on the arms of the chair to trap me in the seat. His mouth curled wider and he closed to within an inch of my face as he murmured, "*I am your Prince Charming, Connie. Haven't you guessed it, yet?*"

His mocking eyes and low chuckle stole my breath. But it was the soft brush of his lips on mine that stopped my heart.

Abruptly he straightened, his face and tone flinty. "You'll stay here. If you try to escape, I promise you'll pay for it."

Our eyes remained locked a small eternity until he pivoted, stalked out, and shut me into my gilded cage.

ONCE MY BODY STOPPED TREMBLING and I knew my legs would hold my weight, I pushed up and looked around. Still a little shaky, I wandered the oak-panelled chamber and pulled the protective coverings to reveal plush chairs separated by small occasional tables, a mirrored vanity, two high dressers with gold fittings, a cheval glass, and twin round night tables—all antiques that gleamed with years of polish. The room smelled of orange wax from furniture and floor, a hint of wood smoke from the fireplace, and the indefinable uniqueness of every stranger's home.

A porcelain chamber-pot rested beneath a chaise percée hidden behind a screen decorated with mother-of-pearl inlaid in an oriental design. I supposed the redundant little privy had been kept for show, since it sat next to the door that led to the private bath sumptuously appointed with snowy fixtures, marble tiles, and golden faucets.

To my relief, toilet paper, towels, and soap had already been provided. Likewise, the bed had been made, as I discovered when I drew back the brocade curtains that matched the golden upholstery of the chairs. I didn't care for the colour, my preference running to greens and blues, but it was not my home, after all, and at least it would be a comfortable prison.

Though I had heard John Crozier, or whoever he was (I doubted that was his real name), insert and turn a key, I tested the doorknob anyway. Then, despite his warning, I tried the windows as well. To my dismay, I noticed little keyholes under the handles. Heaving a resigned sigh, I sauntered back to stare at my image in the mirror. My rumpled and soiled blue pants and blue-and-white checked cotton blouse and dirty hair emphasized my status both as an interloper who did not belong in this monument to wealth and privilege and as a captive whose very life depended on the forbearance and ultimate aims of criminals.

Tremors returning at the thought, I flung the gold-velvet draperies wide and peered out into the early twilight. I could not see below, but I knew each level of the house was unusually tall. Glancing up, I estimated the plaster ceiling to be twelve feet from the floor. And the lower storeys rose even higher, I recalled, making the drop from the window ledge at least thirty-five feet and probably more. My heart sank. A long way to fall, even if I could get the windows open.

Discouraged, I decided to bathe and wash out my clothes. If nothing else, I could meet my fate feeling clean.

WRAPPED IN A SUBSTANTIAL TOWEL of white terrycloth, I wandered the room again, this time opening drawers and inspecting contents. Instead of the silky garments I had hoped for, even if they were ill-fitting, I found only satin linings or bare wood.

A metallic scratch and a click turned me to the door that swung wide to admit Crozier carrying a tray of food. He, too, had bathed, as evidenced by his wet hair and clean scent, and he now sported black denims rather than blue, with a black tee stretched over bulging muscles. As my eyes slid appreciatively over his form while he set the silver salver on the table before the fireplace, an inner voice bemoaned my luck at meeting a gorgeous man who had proven to be yet another stinker.

When he straightened and turned, I wrenched my gaze up to his face and forced a smile in an attempt to cover my wanton musings. But his slow grin and the amused sparkle in his eyes as he approached and lifted a hand to caress my flaming cheek indicated that I could not hide the thoughts that betrayed my none-too-discriminating libido.

"Perhaps later, my dear Connie," he whispered.

My breath caught at a darkening of his eyes, their sudden intensity evincing his own lascivious leanings and piercing me with tantalizing promise that set my lower region atingle.

Out of the blue, his gaze hardened and he stepped back and whirled, reaching to a hip pocket and withdrawing a cell phone.

"What?" he demanded as he lifted it to his ear and strode out to lock me in without another glance my way.

HUNGRY AS I WAS after days of nothing but pre-packaged sandwiches, the steak and potatoes and baby carrots tasted like a little bit of heaven. Apparently one of the guys could cook. I snorted a mirthless chuckle that, though they were as misogynistic and macho as any man I had ever met, they would not have dared to put me in a kitchen full of knives. In fact, they had even pre-cut the steak and given me a spoon instead of a fork.

When I finished my meal, I took the tray to the bathroom and washed the dinnerware. Silly, I suppose, but I couldn't countenance allowing the food to dry on the dishes. I had always hated having to scrape plates and cutlery smeared with rock-solid and tenaciously clinging egg or starch after my brother made himself a midnight snack and left the evidence in his room for days or weeks. (He had never once been required to clean up his own mess.)

I had set the wet china and silver into the tub to dry and opened a cupboard to pull out a fresh towel when I heard a faint tinkle. Something small had fallen. My pulse speeding, I scanned the floor for the wayward object. Spying nothing, I stood and opened the cabinet's doors wide to pull out columns of folded towels, bars of soap, bottles of shampoo and lotion, cans of shaving cream, boxes of tissues, rolls of toilet paper, and jars of unguent. When the shelves were bare, I inspected each with finger and eye.

Nothing.

Discouraged, I restocked the cupboards, making sure to return the items to their original positions. When I got to the towels, I decided to replace them one by one, unfolding and refolding them in hope something useful had been hidden among them.

No such luck.

Only the upper shelf remained open. I stood on tiptoe to reach up and push a jutting box of tissue farther back before closing the last door. My right foot connected with something small and hard. At once, I dropped to my knees and groped along the marble to find the anomaly. My heart again began to pound when my fingers discovered a small chunk of metal that had slid into the crevice between the tiles and the decoratively grooved bottom sill of the cupboard.

A wheeze of near hysteria blasted from my chest when I recognized the shape in my hand: It was a tiny key.

Torn between wild hope and a fear that the key might be made for someone's long forgotten diary, I raced to the nearest window, hastily panned the landscape to assure myself no one would see, and then slid the little rod into the brass-clad hole on the wooden casement. When it slid home, I twisted.

Click.

Expelling in a burst the breath I had held, I grasped the handle and tugged. With a little reluctance likely owing to months of disuse, the wood pulled away with a slight creak of the hinges. Instantly, a cool breeze lifted the hair at my temples and I inhaled deeply of the air perfumed with what I guessed to be one of those exotic flowers for which the south was famous. Cherry blossoms, maybe.

At a voice somewhere below, I carefully shut the window and locked it again.

Tonight, I decided. I would wait until well

after dark. Maybe, just maybe, I could climb down the side of the building and run for help.

STILL IN THE TOWEL, not wishing to be completely naked in case one of the men decided to come in and look under the covers, I slid between the sheets and pulled the comforter to my chin. Of course, I realized, if one of them *did* come to avail himself, a towel would not deter him from his intentions. But at least I did not feel like an open invitation as I lay there.

Footfalls passed softly along the hallway and a door opened nearby. Another door closed farther on. I waited.

As I stared into the darkness above, listening in the stillness for an approach, it struck me as odd that these men had access to an empty mansion. And what were they waiting for? How long would they stay here before they continued with whatever they planned?

My eyes fluttered and I stirred, blinking wide and trying to stay awake. But I must have dozed despite efforts to evade Morpheus, for I started and glanced about anxiously, wondering what had caught my attention. When no sounds alerted me and my heart slowed from gallop to walk, I peeled away the coverings and slid out of bed to pad silently to the bathroom. There, after using the facilities, I tossed the towel over the edge of the tub and slipped into the clothes that were still damp but no longer sopping.

On my return to the bedroom, I listened at the door for any indication of danger. Finally, I retrieved the key from where I had hidden it in a drawer of the vanity and dashed to a window to peek out and scan for movement in the light of the rising half-moon. Shadows of trees and shrubs might have hidden anything from a cat to a bear, but I dared to hope that my failure to spot motion was a good sign. Not at all certain this was a good idea, I nonetheless unlocked and opened the window and peeked out to check the lawns of the mansion for a patrolling guard.

After a minute or so by my admittedly poor reckoning, I thrust one leg out over the sill into the night air to sit astride. Holding the jamb, I leaned to feel along the outer wall for hand- and footholds. The stone was rough and the mortar joints were wide enough for my fingers, so I glanced down to estimate how far I would have to climb. My heart skipped.

I straightened in the long opening, closed my eyes tightly, and forcibly calmed my breath.

Then, avoiding a second dizzying look down, I gripped the sill, twisted, found a foothold, and gingerly pulled my other leg out to settle upon a slight jut of stone.

It took another minute or so to calm my respirations and wipe the perspiration from my hands, one at a time, before I risked stretching my stronger leg to find a lower purchase. Why my stronger leg? No idea. Just seemed sensible at the time.

The rough stone abraded my fingertips and taxed the strength of my hands as the ungenerous protrusions of the stone blocks taxed the strength of my legs. Nonetheless, I proceeded downward, albeit at a snail's pace and with several sideways shifts to avoid the windows below.

By the time my feet touched grass, I was soaked with sweat. My knees weak and my hands shaking visibly, I paused to lean against the base of the wall and wait for my pulse and respirations to settle. Finally, I turned away to head for the woods.

But I stopped short, eyes wide and heart in my throat.

CHAPTER 8

Netted

HE NEEDED ONLY ONE STEP to reach me and grab my nape with one hand as he seized my waist and pinned me to him with the other. He hissed at my ear, "It's time for you to show me why I should keep you alive, Connie."

With that, he clutched the back of my head and smothered my lips in a savage, bruising kiss. When his hold eased slightly and he pulled back, I saw the rage flashing in his eyes and the snarl contorting his mouth as he shoved me to the ground. I had not even time to roll before he pounced to trap me under his weight.

"I told you this would cost you," he said as he sat back on his haunches, quickly unbuckled his belt, and unfastened his jeans.

I lay breathless and mesmerized while he snatched off his tee and then ripped at my blouse, popping buttons and rending fabric as he bared my chest and then moved on to expose my lower half and his. Part of me was horrified at the prospect of being raped. But another part wanted this man more than I had ever wanted a man before, and my nether engorged and moistened at the imminent fulfillment of a primal urge.

There was no foreplay. He slammed my wrists into the grass above my head and plunged into me with a ferocity that might have torn flesh had that primitive hunger I had tried in vain to suppress not welcomed his invasion. Relentless rhythmic pounding wrested gasps from my lips as his eyes held mine captive, the two of us locked in a mindless dance of dominance and submission. Gradually, a need awakened in me and grew stronger with his every thrust. My hips strained toward his and my throat uttered eager cries at his ongoing assault. Above me, his eyes now gleamed with a barbarous avidity and the curl of his mouth morphed from cruelty to triumph.

All at once, a dam burst inside me and the release threw me into convulsions of pleasure such as I had never experienced. My reaction triggered his climax, and soon we were panting together under the moonlight, our bodies still conjoined.

At that moment, I, for one, could not have stood up much less run away.

As if to mock me, the low rumble of a car rolled by in the distance and a bird flew overhead in silent freedom, the visible stars winking off and then on again to mark its passage. The immediate smells of sweat and male lust almost masking the cloying fragrance that pervaded the atmosphere, and the pounding of Crozier's heart against my breast as I lay trapped beneath him further taunted me. I closed my eyes on a sigh, not sure whether to laugh or cry.

A little while later, he pushed up and collapsed beside me on the grass. Respirations yet laboured, he rolled to his back and began to chuckle softly. I turned my head to regard him. Finally, he settled and looked to me with something that, in another man, might have been fondness.

"You are the damnedest woman," was all he said.

HE LET ME DRESS—as best I could with half my buttons missing—before he dragged me by the wrist into the house and up the stairs. After propelling me into the bedroom once more, he glanced to the open window and then fixed my eyes with a cold stare.

"Next time," he said quietly, "I'll let Joaquin have you. And I guarantee you won't enjoy it."

He held my gaze a long moment before he whirled about, exited, and locked the door.

Alone again in my cage, I hugged myself and shivered, unwilling, or perhaps unable, to imagine anything outside of this suite and this day.

CHAPTER 9

Fish-bowl

MARTY BROUGHT BREAKFAST. Arrogant and curt as he was, at least I did not have to deal with Joaquin. The idea of being alone with the Latino even for a few minutes gave me the willies. That he might decide he had time for more than tossing a plate of food before me turned my stomach. I didn't know his story, and I didn't want to. Whatever had moulded him into a vicious woman-hater, I could only hope he would have no opportunity to take out his rage on me. Or anyone else, for that matter.

With nothing better to do after washing the dishes, I dug out the books I had found in the bottom drawer of the vanity. One was an ancient copy of Jane Austen's *Sense and Sensibility*. Another was a venerable collection of Shakespearean plays. And a smaller and much more modern volume contained poems by Robert Frost. Figuring my time here would be limited to a few more days at most, I opted for the last and moved one of the wingchairs closer to the window in order to read by daylight.

Rain began to patter against the sill. I stood and closed the casement just as the door opened behind me. At the sound, I whirled to find Crozier eyeing me with one brow high.

"Going somewhere?"

"Keeping out the rain," I replied.

He tilted his head and stared at me a long moment. Finally, he closed the door and gestured toward the bed with one hand as he began to unbuckle his belt with the other.

Wanting to preserve what was left of my garments, if not my dignity, I hastily shrugged them off and tossed them onto the wing chair before throwing back the covers and slipping into bed. Lying there, I watched as he slowly undressed all the while he watched me watching him.

I warmed and moistened at memory of the sensations experienced the night before.

HE TOOK HIS TIME in a leisurely exploration of my body that aroused me in a way entirely different from the angry ravishment of our first encounter, yet one even more stimulating. By the time I reached orgasm, I thought my heart would explode. And he, too, lay at my side a long while afterward, drained as well as sated.

He said nothing, though his gaze held a peculiar light I could not identify as he surveyed the full-body blush that had resulted from his handiwork. I stared back, equally loth to shatter the spell that bound us in a fragile universe of pleasure that could evaporate at the merest disturbance.

Finally, with a faint smile that seemed to hold a hint of sadness, he rolled off the mattress, dressed, and left without looking back.

Perhaps as much as a half-hour later, I rose and ambled to the bathroom to bathe.

IT WENT ON LIKE THAT day after day, with Crozier spending a few hours of passion with me each afternoon and a few more in the night. Marty brought meals and looked me up and down suggestively, but he made no move and I suspected that Crozier had claimed me as his own. For the time being, at least.

I tried not to think of the future. I might not have one.

CHAPTER 10

Open seas

I HAD FINISHED *Sense and Sensibility* by the time I realized I had seen no one for at least a day. My stomach growled to remind me I had not been fed in that time, either. Putting down the book, I stood and went to the window to see what might be seen.

Nothing. Just scudding clouds and wind whipping foliage.

I strode to the door and knocked.

"Is anybody there?" I yelled. "I'm

hungry."

No answer.

I tried the knob, but of course it wouldn't budge.

After drinking from the bathroom faucet and pacing for what must surely have been a half-hour, I yelled at the door again. When no hint of response came, I tried shouting out the window. Again, no sign of life.

Finally, I decided to take a chance and defy Crozier's order. I climbed out the window.

I SLUMPED AT THE BASE OF THE WALL for several minutes before I pushed up on shaky legs to walk around to the nearest entrance. Unfortunately, the nearest was the double front door and it was locked. So I heaved a sigh and trudged on around to the postern. I frowned as I surveyed the courtyard along the way: The truck had disappeared.

The back door opened easily and I stepped in to find no one inside. A pile of dishes cluttered the sink and the coffeepot sat empty.

"Hello?" I called, and suddenly wondered why on earth I was looking for my captors instead of trying to get away to freedom. A jumbled mass of images, most of them featuring Crozier, crowded my mind in a response that left me doubting my sanity.

"Well, I'm hungry," I muttered, and I opened a door that, as I had hoped, led to a pantry. There was a single heel of bread in a wooden box, but the rest of the items were staples that would require combination and culinary skill to turn into a meal; so, I checked out the refrigerator I had spotted. To my relief, I found juice, eggs, butter, and a few other odds and ends that would produce a fine breakfast. I set to work and made myself a small feast.

A while later, my belly full and all the dishes washed and set in the drain rack, I left the kitchen to explore the mansion. Room after room proved empty, and my belly grew more and more taut as I came to suspect I was utterly alone, here. I had even inspected the attic and the outbuildings by the time the sun began to set and my stomach demanded attention again.

Returning to the kitchen, I tossed the few remaining vegetables and some water into a pan for soup, spiced it, and set it to simmer while I made a batch of biscuits. I had eaten my solitary meal and cleaned up once more when I heard the old clock by the front entry strike eleven.

For the first time since discovering I was, effectively, free, I wondered what I should do. Should I call police? Should I borrow one of the bicycles I had seen in the garage and get to a town, first? Should I just walk away?

My gut tightened again as I wondered what had happened to Crozier and his friends. And I realized I was probably suffering from that Stockholm syndrome I had once heard about, that I had come to depend on my kidnappers to such a degree that a part of me wanted to continue the relationship. Certainly, I could not deny that I missed one captor in particular: my Prince Charming.

Eyes welling with the confusion that muddled my mind, I had started toward the stairs to go to bed when I heard a car approaching at high speed. I ran to the door and out into the courtyard as a black Mercedes squealed to a halt. Its door flew open and Crozier unfolded to step out.

He stopped dead at sight of me. Then, with a spasm of laughter, he loped forward and grabbed me up into his arms to plant a hungry kiss. But he cut it short and set me down with a glance toward the road.

"I have no time," he said. He wrenched

free the hem of his pale cotton shirt bloused over dark slacks to expose a money belt. With a shriek of Velcro, he tore it away from his midsection and handed it to me. "Here. Go home."

I blinked in bewilderment. "What?"

"Go home," he repeated. "You don't need to worry about Marty or Joaquin; they're dead. And you're free."

With a quick, rough kiss, he darted back to the car, slid in, slammed the door, turned on the engine, and roared around in a tight circle to race away down the drive and out onto the road. I stood staring after him, watching the white of the headlight beams and the red of the taillights disappear.

When the moon rose above the treetops, I scanned the empty courtyard, rubbed my chilly arms, and wandered back into the house. Upstairs, I found an open bedroom that smelled of him and crawled into the unmade bed to cry myself to sleep.

MY PURSE HAD BEEN LEFT IN THE VAN, I remembered as I fixed breakfast with what remained of the perishables. I had no identification of any kind and would likely end up arrested at the border if I tried to cross. So, simply heading north was not advisable. I mulled long and hard, hoping to think of an alternative to the one option that kept presenting itself.

Reluctantly, as the clock struck nine, I fastened my ragged blouse with safety pins I'd found in a kitchen drawer, packed the leftover biscuits for lunch, closed up the mansion as best I could, and set out for the nearest town. Travelling on foot, I quickly came to the attention of a patrol car and, after describing my predicament, I landed in a police station where more explanations were demanded. No doubt a team was sent to the estate and calls made to verify my strange story, while I sat and told and retold it to a detective whose arched brows and unblinking stare made it clear he thought I was lying to cover a crime or high on a street drug.

Eventually, the officers must have decided I might be telling the truth and I was granted a phone call to the embassy. After explaining again and again to one department and another and spending over a half-hour, in between, on hold while embassy staff figured out who my call should be routed to, I finally found someone willing to listen to the whole tale. An hour later, I climbed into a car sent courtesy of my government.

A long night of even more explanations and paperwork followed. It seemed every functionary in the embassy and more from various American agencies wanted to hear my story. I left out details, of course, including mention of the money belt. (I may be a dim bulb, but I'm not totally benighted.) But they only wanted to know what I recalled of the events leading to my kidnapping, a description of the route the truck followed, and all I knew of the men involved in the conspiracy.

My eyes were drooping and I had become incoherent by the time someone decided I should sleep awhile. A young woman with a French accent showed me to a modest lounge and covered me when I curled up on a couch. I don't recall hearing her leave.

I WOKE TO THE SMELL OF COFFEE. Squinting at the brilliant light pouring through a picture window with its curtains thrown wide, I panned the casually fashionable surroundings that managed to be comfortable while also totally devoid of personality. A vaguely familiar form hovered over a nearby table. I gaped when Graham Urquhart turned around with a mug in each hand and smiled at me.

"Hi, Connie."

"Graham! What are you doing here?"

"Following you," he said brightly as though it were the most natural thing in the world.

I shifted upright, and he sat next to me and handed me a mug.

"I don't understand. How could you do that?"

"Remember that keychain I gave you?"

I thought back to our first visit to an art gallery and his thoughtful gift of a key ring with a little timepiece attached. My hesitant smile no doubt expressed lingering bafflement.

He explained, "It had a locator in it."

I stared at him through narrowed eyes. "What? Why?"

His tone and manner were purely conversational. "Your communication with a certain foreign dignitary—or rather, someone purporting to be Prince Ali bin Rashid bin Amin Al ash-Sheikh—came to our attention and we monitored you." With a hand up in a halting gesture, he added, "Not just you. There were several others contacted. But when your messages continued while others stopped, we knew they were concentrating on you."

"You thought I was one of them," I assumed with alarm.

"No," Graham assured me with a shake of his head. "We gathered they were manipulating you. But we had trouble tracking your communications: They were using very sophisticated methods to cloak their origins and to scramble messages even over what should have been regular channels. So, we decided our best bet was to keep an eye on you personally. That's why as soon as your signed your lease I arranged to move in next to you and I bugged your laptop."

With an apologetic grimace, he leaned in to say, "I'm sorry about the repair expense. I'll see you're reimbursed."

Again I gaped, nonplussed at the revelation I had been under such close scrutiny. Then, I frowned. "Wait a minute. If you were keeping an eye on me, how is it you didn't rescue me long since?"

At that, he blushed and chewed his lip a moment before he confessed, "I wanted to, but my superiors—and the American authorities—

insisted on proof of the connection between the men who kidnapped you and certain members of the American government." In the tone of an aside, he said, "Both our governments had got wind of a plot some months ago."

His face contorting with embarrassed dismay, he admitted further, "And, to be honest, we lost you a couple of times because of interference with the signal from your purse—which, by the way, is why we didn't know you were at the estate. That and the fact we didn't realize you had become separated from your bag. When we picked up the signal on the move, we assumed they kept you close as a potential hostage."

It occurred to me at that moment that if Crozier and his cronies had tossed my handbag before we got to the border, they might have succeeded in their mission.

"That reminds me," I said, "what were they planning to do? I never heard them talk about it." At a flashed image of that fateful night at Donnegan's, I wondered anxiously, "And what happened to Hal and Gino? Are they okay?"

"You mean the guards at the trucking company?"

I nodded confirmation.

He smiled. "They're fine. There were traces of a sedative in their coffee. The man you know as Crozier doesn't kill indiscriminately." He frowned. "Though, I'm surprised he let you go when you can testify against him on a kidnapping charge if we manage to capture the bastard."

Sobering, Graham added, "As to your earlier question, that you will never know. It's highly classified and I'm not allowed to tell you."

"Oh." I sighed. "Figures. I nearly get killed, and I don't even get to know what it was all about."

Graham patted my hand. "Just as well. Some things you're better off not knowing. Trust me: There are truths that can keep you awake at night."

Noting something in his eyes that suggested he spoke from experience, I nodded solemn acceptance. Then, I pouted my lips cheekily and regarded him. "So...I'm guessing you don't work for Revenue Canada."

He threw back his head and laughed.

CHAPTER 11

Swimming upstream

AS I HAD EXPECTED Bill fired me, albeit with some reluctance because, apart from my one serious and costly lapse in judgement, I had been a good worker. In exchange for a favourable reference, he exacted my promise never to get involved with any online Romeos again. I couldn't blame him for imposing the condition.

Unfortunately, jobs were as scarce in the city as in the smaller towns. After pounding the pavement for several weeks, I decided to head north again. At least the cost of living would be slightly less outside the urban centre.

My home town was out because Jean-Guy still lived there. As did my other exes. But the money Crozier had unexpectedly handed me allowed me to buy an almost-new car and a former farmhouse on a back-country lane.

Normally, taking on a neglected two-storey house and a three-acre parcel that lay, effectively, in the middle of nowhere would have been a bizarre choice as well as a foolish one. But unbeknownst to me at the time, my nesting instincts had influenced my decision. Most of my boxes were still unpacked when I finally noticed that my menstrual period was long overdue and my waist had outgrown my cool-weather clothing.

"Great!" I groused as I tossed onto the bed the corduroys I had planned to wear to go into the nearby town for my shift at the diner. I plopped down next to the pile of discarded slacks and closed my eyes. Although I had not felt the morning sickness proclaimed by book and movie to be a sure sign of pregnancy, I knew that some women never experience discomfort prior to giving birth. I resigned myself to the need to pick up a home pregnancy test. And the likelihood I would lose another job.

    The Welfare rolls beckoned.

I WADDLED TO MY DESK and set down my mug of coffee before I sat heavily in the swivel chair and turned to the screen. A glance out the curtainless window on my left told me the snowstorm had not let up. Good thing I had no place to go, today.

    Thanking the universe for that bit of luck, I looked back to the monitor. Now that blogging had become my main source of income, albeit a spare one, I usually worked six days a week from early morning to mid afternoon. My routine might need to change come spring, when gardening to grow as much as possible of my food supply would best be done before the heat of the day made such labour unbearable. But for now, I could live in my loose, comfy flannelette pyjamas and woollen robe while I scoured the net for ideas and information to transform into posts for my own website. And if I stank for not having showered for a couple of days, there was no one to notice but me.

    I flicked the power switch, entered my password, and sipped my black brew as I waited for the computer to boot up. Once I had run a security scan, I opened my browser and navigated to my e-mail accounts, each in turn, to skim through the newsletters and personal messages that had accumulated since the day before.

I frowned when I came to an e-card. It was neither my birthday nor a special occasion; so, why had someone sent me a card?

The sender was also a puzzle: someone by the name of Ian Cross. Not one of my subscribers.

Figuring it was probably misdirected because of a typo in the address, I opened it expecting to reply in order to let the man know his missive had gone astray.

"Sweet Connie," it read.

I sucked a shocked breath. Then, I swallowed and continued to read with pulse in overdrive.

"It pleases me to see you well. Your choice of home is unexpected, but not without merit. Nonetheless, you will need assistance to care for our child. For that reason, I have set up a digital-currency account for you. Follow this link to complete the process. I have also added to your Paypal wallet. And you will find your bank balance has increased as well.

"I regret that there is nothing else I can offer you. Not even further communication.

"Ian"

Tears flooded my cheeks as I hurried to the front door and out onto the porch. I stood long in the cold, searching through the driven flakes for any sign of him. But no manly shape and no movement marred the white landscape and white sky. Finally, chilled to the bone, I plodded into my empty house and closed the door.

GRAHAM URQUHART REGARDED ME, fingering the mug I had placed before him and that he had subsequently drained while chattering about the weather and avoiding the real reason for his visit. I held his gaze.

After a long moment of silence, he assured me, "I'm not concerned about the money. I know you need it and I can't blame you for doing whatever it takes to steer clear of government assistance and the red tape that goes with it." With a wry smile, he qualified, "Well, anything short of actual crime, that is."

I made no reply. He had never told me what department he worked for, but I guessed he was part of the Intelligence community. That meant he probably had access to financial information of every kind, with the possible exception of cash-under-the-table transactions.

His mouth worked a moment. Finally, he said, "If he contacts you again, we'd like to know."

My left brow arched high. "Since you already know he contacted me, which means you have access to my e-mails, I expect you'll know before I do in the unlikely event he sends another message."

With a pointed glance toward my swollen belly, Graham suggested, "He might do more than send money or mail."

My smile sad, I replied, "Let's not kid ourselves, Graham. He's not that kind of man."

The agent's rueful expression contained the merest hint of pity and his slow nod acknowledged my assessment.

CHAPTER 12

Home waters

PUDGY LITTLE PAWS patted the soil around the transplant. I watched as my son set his hands more firmly upon the loam and lifted his diapered bum into the air before pushing up to teeter on bare feet and unsteady legs in the garden bed. His black hair gleamed in the morning sunlight and his clear blue eyes sparkled with delight at his accomplishment. Nothing elicited squeals of joy like playing in the dirt and learning to tend the greenery.

I smiled happily as he turned and propelled himself onto the grassy path to run to the tray of seedlings waiting their turn to be placed in their permanent home. He fell to his hands and knees three times on that two-metre stretch, but he instantly leapt up each time, determined to reach his destination.

When he looked back at me expectantly, I sauntered over and bent to pick up a tiny plant potted in newsprint and gently set it into the tyke's eager hands. Together, we returned to the open spot I had loosened before breakfast, and he deposited another baby tomato in the sun-kissed soil.

Observing fondly, I marvelled that the plump skin, bare except at his bottom, had already warmed from pale cream to honey beige.

So like his father.

THE DREAM CAME AGAIN, all fire and passion that could only end in frustration. I sighed as my eyes fluttered open to be greeted by darkness.

Something brushed my lips and heat emanated from close by my side. My brows furrowed as I turned toward a large form black against a slightly lighter murk behind. The mattress felt...wrong. It dipped as though under a weight greater than my own.

The blackness loomed nearer, blotting out the hint of dawn that paled the window. Heat pressed in and a gentle breeze blew across my face just as my lips again felt the merest trace of a caress.

My eyes flew wide at the kiss that followed, a firm mouth meeting mine. A familiar mouth. And a scent that set my heart thumping wildly. Was I still dreaming?

I dared not speak lest the phantom evaporate and leave me once more in a living hell of desperate longing. Silently, I reached out to stroke the incarnation of my desires, praying that it would remain substantial for a little while.

Only when we lay together, still locked in carnal embrace and panting with the power of climax, did I risk breaking the spell.

"John? Or is it Ian?" I whispered.

"Shh," he responded with a forefinger to my lips. "I can't stay, sweet Connie. Nor could I stay away, as mad as that is."

He pulled back, and in the growing light I discerned the chiselled features and bright eyes I had come to love. Brushing away a strand of my hair, he murmured, "You've crawled under my skin, you silly woman, and I can't get you out." On an exhalation, he said, "You'll be the death of me."

His mouth curved wryly and he leaned to kiss me before pulling me into his arms to press my cheek to his chest. "Sleep now," he commanded softly.

"I WOKE ALONE, but his scent on the rumpled sheets assured me he had been here in the flesh."

I glanced to each of my sons and my daughter, the former sober in gray suits and black armbands, the latter in deep purple, and all so much like their father my heart ached at sight of their jet hair, cerulean eyes, and strikingly beautiful features.

"He came back twice more. Each time, he stayed a few days before he vanished again." My wistful smile widened. "But he left more than money behind."

"I think I remember him," said Sean, nodding reflectively. "I thought he was a giant."

I grinned as I looked up to where he towered over me. "You inherited the giant gene."

We all snickered, for I was the runt of our

family. When the laughter died, I inhaled deeply, opened the urn of pure gold, and upended it over the ravine that edged my property.

For several minutes, we stood in silence, staring down into the leaf-choked gully. Finally, we strolled back through the woods toward the house for the official reading of the Will.

As we approached the back porch, I spotted a grizzled Graham Urquhart standing by a grey car on the opposite side of the road, his expression...guilty. I looked away without acknowledgement as I continued on, all the while I saw in my mind the final message from my Prince Charming.

FROM: RICHARD BLACK, AKA IAN CROSS, AKA JOHN CROZIER, AKA ALI
To: Connie Tyson
Subject: For the record
Sweet Connie,

This message is, no doubt, unwise. Nevertheless I choose to send it.

There is something I must do: one more job before I retire to a secluded island with no extradition treaties. But for the first time I am not certain of the outcome. Specifically, I am not sure

I will survive.

For that reason, I have made certain arrangements. In the event of my death, you will receive instructions from a lawyer by the name of Hamish MacPherson, a Scot of Edinburgh. He will execute my Last Will and Testament. There are few men I have ever trusted, but I know he will do all I have asked.

I never wanted to love you. In truth, I did not expect to love anyone, for I thought love a foolish illusion—nothing more than a whitewashing of lust. But you kept surprising me with unexpected courage and honest compassion when I've known only a world full of greedy, selfish cowards. Perhaps I'm one of the latter. I suppose I am. Yet I found myself drawn to you, and my lascivious desires competed with something I had never before felt: admiration and, even more astounding, a possessive need to protect you. So, I kept you alive when expedience dictated I should kill you. Then, I curbed my pleasures in order to provide for you and the children. And I risked capture to be with you or, on occasion, just to catch a glimpse of you—absurd as that seems.

My sons and daughter are like you, and that I can only attribute to the influence of their kind, patient, and loving mother. I am proud of them and I am proud of you.

I do not judge myself so generously—which is a further indication of the mark you have made upon me, for before we met I had always considered my own actions justified, whatever benefited me the highest good, and definitions of "character" mere pseudo-religious manipulation of the masses. But I am what I am, and if there is a God, after all, I will have many crimes to answer for.

Whatever the outcome of my final job, we will never meet again. Perhaps it is my vanity and arrogance that assures me you will not forget me, though of course I have left four reminders.

For my own part, I will never be free of you.

I will say this only once: I love you.
Farewell, sweet Connie.
Richard

ACKNOWLEDGEMENTS

I thank all who have encouraged me in my writing and all who have helped along the way.

Special thanks go to Draft2Digital.com for making both digital and print versions of my books possible.

Reviews help readers find new books they may enjoy. So, if you liked this story, please post a review on your favourite retail or review site.

Other Books by Allison M. Azulay

Twin Romance Series

Propositions and Proposals
Fates and Furies

Standalone Stories

The Chalice of Forever

Coffee Break Anthologies

That Christmas Feeling
In Heaven and Earth
Fateful Attractions

about the author

Stories of all kinds enthralled Allison M. Azulay when she was a child, starting with fairy tales read aloud by her parents. Since that time, she has devoured everything from romance and historical drama, to mysteries and crime thrillers, to chick lit and science fiction.

Though she wrote tales of her own in her youth, "adulting" put a damper on her creativity awhile.

Later, encouraged by her husband, she explored her talents and now writes romance and adventure novels and short stories, for the most part, though she dabbles in other genres as well.

"I try to give readers the sorts of emotional thrills I get from reading books by Diana Gabaldon and Diana Palmer.